"Sam, what are you doing to me?"

Hopefully driving him half as wild as he was driving her. With Jack standing so close, cupping her face with his big hands, avoiding a dance had become the last thing on her mind. "I should mention—" Sam sank her teeth into his earlobe, thrilling to the sound that dragged from him "—it's been a little too long for me. I'm liking this way too much."

"Don't tell me that." His hand skimmed up her back, while the other rested on her hip. His thumb glided over her belly, then moved upward, stroking each rib as it climbed. He traced her last rib, then just barely touched the bottom curve of her breast.

All the while his gaze held her, conveying hunger, passion, desire...more heady than the champagne she'd sipped. She let out a shuddery breath.

Then his thumb made another sweep, not quite touching her nipple, and she had to concentrate on breathing.

Sinking her fingers into his hair, she brought his mouth back to hers, and their moans mingled, becoming part of the crazy, wild kiss.

Dear Reader,

I've always wanted to be a surfer girl. I grew up in L.A. in the fun and sun, but alas, I was never coordinated enough to make it on a surfboard. So I created a heroine who was. Samantha O'Ryan—Sam to her friends—is one tough cookie. She's had to be. Surfing in the mornings, running her little café in the afternoons, she thinks she has it all.

Enter one Jack Knight, ex-basketball star and current rich bum. After a life in the limelight, all he wants is peace and quiet. But then these two are thrown together by one well-meaning nosy older sister, a fancy charity event complete with obnoxious paparazzi, and a dunking booth.

Oh, and throw in a red-hot, undeniable attraction like nothing either Sam or Jack have ever experienced. Watch them both fall hard. Hope you do, too.

Best wishes and happy reading,

Jill Shalvis

Books by Jill Shalvis

Seduce Me
JILL SHALVIS

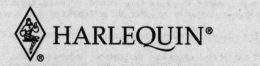

HARLEQUIN®

TORONTO • NEW YORK • LONDON
AMSTERDAM • PARIS • SYDNEY • HAMBURG
STOCKHOLM • ATHENS • TOKYO • MILAN • MADRID
PRAGUE • WARSAW • BUDAPEST • AUCKLAND

To my very own future basketball stars

ISBN 0-373-69195-5

SEDUCE ME

Copyright © 2004 by Jill Shalvis.

www.eHarlequin.com

Printed in U.S.A.

1

SAMANTHA O'RYAN had been eyeing half-naked, wet, glistening men for hours under the guise of teaching them to surf. They'd offered to pay her but, truthfully, she'd gotten the most out of the deal. She just loved being in the water, on her board. After she finished giving the group of college kids pointers, she walked down the beach and up the stairs to let herself into her outdoor café, where she went to work on her second love—creating fun, exotic sandwiches.

As she served her customers, she realized she had no plans after work, her favorite kind of evening. She could bodysurf by moonlight if she chose, or drive up Pacific Coast Highway as far as a tank of gas would take her…anything.

That was the beauty of being unencumbered.

Although she wouldn't mind being temporarily encumbered—for a night, that is. It had been a long dry spell without a guy around.

Her own fault.

"You sold everything." Lorissa Barrett, her best friend and part-time server at the Wild Cherries café, looked surprised as she surveyed the empty display cases at the cash register. "Well, except the brownies. You make terrible brownies."

"Hey, thanks."

But Lorissa was right. Everything but the brownies were gone, including the new turkey-with-mango-spread special. Sam could drum up inventive stuff like that with ease, bake the most mouthwatering cookies on the planet, but she failed at brownies every single time. She knew why; she just didn't like to think about it.

"Sorry." Looking anything but, Lorissa leaned against the counter, her amusement slowly fading.

"Uh-oh," Sam said. "What is it?"

"Nothing."

They had a long history and knew each other better than anyone else did. "If it's nothing, then stop staring at me like you're trying to get your nerve up for *something*."

"I'm not."

Sam shrugged and turned back to cleaning the countertop.

Lorissa sighed. "Okay, I have this favor."

"Pass." It was a hot one today, and Sam swiped at her forehead, then dusted off the display cases.

"You can't turn down a favor when you don't

even know what it is." Lorissa tossed back her long, red, wildly curly hair and pushed out her full, highly glossed lower lip in a pout that was extremely effective on men, but not on Sam.

"Sure I can. In fact, I just did." Sam moved outside to the bright red plastic tables, wiping them down, lowering their red-and-white-striped umbrellas, all the while watching the sun slowly sink into the glorious Pacific Ocean. "When you ask for a favor in the same tone you might mention a funeral, I know better than to even hesitate." Sam stretched out the muscles in her neck and back, and thought a midnight swim later tonight might be just the thing she needed, especially in lieu of a man.

"You could at least let me tell you what the favor is."

"I do *not* want a blind date," Sam said emphatically.

Lorissa rolled her eyes. "The way you read my mind really creeps me out."

"It doesn't take a psychic. You've got a hot new fling going with that rich Cole guy, and he keeps asking you to set up his friends with your friends."

"I'm sorry. This is what happens when you're my *bestest* friend."

"Flattery will get you nowhere." Sam shifted to the covered patio area and checked the tables there. All clean. "You know I've been quite patient through all the hideous blind dates you've set me up with over the years. I'm not interested in trying another."

"They haven't all been hideous."

"I have two words for you—Toe Guy."

"Okay, that one can be explained. I forgot your weird foot fetish, and how was I supposed to know about his accident with the lawn mower?"

"I don't want a date tonight."

"Good. Because it's for tomorrow night."

Sam walked back inside to the kitchen and looked around, cleaning up as she went. All she needed to do now was shut off the lights and she was done. She could head out…or simply go upstairs, where she had a nice little apartment. Little being the key word, of course, but she liked little, and the place was her own. She'd made it so. "I'm busy tomorrow night."

"Please, Sam. One date, that's all I'm asking." Lorissa batted her long lashes over her light caramel eyes. "Cole promises me this guy is rich."

"And yet he can't get his own date." Sam hit the switches and the main part of the café went dark. She locked the small kitchen and pulled the retractable gate around the patio area. "What's wrong with that picture, Lorissa?"

"Listen." Lorissa pressed her fingers to her temples, closing her eyes for a second. When she opened them, they were filled with emotion. "I really like this one, Sammie."

Sam took a good look at her. She'd known Lorissa twenty-odd years, since kindergarten. Together, they'd already been through so much: Lorissa's parents' nasty divorce, her mother's suicide when they'd been twelve, and a close friend's overdose at age thirteen. Then Sam losing her parents in a car wreck on the night of their eighth-grade graduation. Between them they'd racked up more mileage on the road of life than most others their age.

And they'd survived, each in her own way. Lorissa had stayed with her father and his new wife, trying junior college in San Diego but deciding higher learning wasn't for her. Now, she drew caricatures on the beach and was good enough to make a decent living at the local weekend Malibu craft fairs. She supplemented this income by serving weekdays at Wild Cherries—when she wasn't busy surfing.

As for Sam, she'd gone to live with Red, her mother's beach-bum brother, who'd had no more idea of what to do with a hurting kid than how to cope with his own grief. The car accident that had killed her parents had been her father's fault and by the time the dust had settled years later, Sam was left with little money. She'd already begun working at Red's place, Wild Cherries. Happy enough to have her friends, she'd lived in the moment—surfing in the mornings, working a shift for cranky uncle Red in the afternoons…an easy career choice.

During the few times she let herself think too much, she remembered her motto: Enjoy every little thing as it happens, appreciate all of it. She repeated that mantra often, because she knew that if she ever acknowledged all she'd been through, she'd drown. As a coping mechanism, it had worked.

And as the years passed, little changed. Red retired, and Sam scrimped, saved and went into debt to buy the business from him. Now, at twenty-six, things were good. Maybe she didn't often engage her emotions, but she didn't want to. She recognized that about herself and was smart enough to know she couldn't even skim that pool; it simply went too deep.

Like Sam, Lorissa also had commitment issues. For her to date a man more than once was rare, much less admit she really liked him. "You sure about this Cole guy?" Sam asked Lorissa now. "You know how rich guys are. They're like the too-good-looking ones—they always turn out to be jerks."

"Not this one." Lorissa's smile was earnest.

"Please, Sam. Just one little date. Just one short night out of your life—"

"Yeah." She was still shocked at Lorissa's willingness to fall for Cole. "Fine."

"—It won't be so bad, and you can call me from your cell phone every few minutes. If you need me, I'll come up with a way to rescue you, I promise. I—"

"I said fine."

"I'll give you—"

"Lor, honey, *I'll do it.*"

Lorissa blinked and gave a slow, relieved smile. "Really?"

"But I swear to you, if he's got hair plugs or garlic breath or tries to cop a feel, I'm outta there."

Lorissa beamed. "Deal."

Great. Deal. Sam turned away from the café and looked at the ocean. Four- to five-footers pounded the surf. A jogger made his way down the sand, along with a few other stragglers. For a hot late August evening, the place was quiet. "Let's go for a swim."

Lorissa checked her watch, something she rarely did. In fact, Sam couldn't believe she was even wearing a watch. "I've got an hour before I'm catching up with Cole."

"You've been late since the day you were born. Why the sudden concern with being on time?"

"I'm meeting his parents."

Sam did a double take. *Parents?* That sounded...
real, and she suddenly took this whole thing more
seriously. "Hasn't it only been a week?"

"Yes, but it seems like a lifetime," Lorissa said
with a dreamy sigh.

As they walked to the water, Sam got all protective. "What does he do again?"

"He's in marketing."

"Marketing." How...vague. Her bikini was already under her sundress as usual, which she
stripped off and Lorissa did the same.

"You're going to love him, I promise," Lorissa
said.

Sam would see about that. Privately, she was already prepared to hate the guy who'd captured
her best friend's heart. He'd better treat her right,
or she'd—

"Which reminds me..." Lorissa grimaced.
"There's sort of a stipulation about your date."

"Stipulation?"

"The guy is a client of Cole's, as well as a friend.
The deal is you go with him to some big fancy
charity event—"

"Whoa. Dressing up?"

"Yes, dressing up. You make nice at the charity
dinner and auction, and you can't talk to the
press."

"Who *is* this guy?" Sam pictured some smarmy, overly sophisticated businessman gone Hollywood.

"Just remember, *rich*."

"Great."

"So you agree to the terms? The no talking to the press thing?" Lorissa shot her a worried look. "Since you've never been fond of the press anyway, it shouldn't be a problem, right?"

Tomorrow night was going to be one long exercise in patience. Not that Sam had anything against dating. The opposite, actually. She enjoyed going out and meeting men.

But a guy she hadn't picked, laying down rules…it all just went against the grain somehow. And yet, there Lorissa stood in her yellow bikini and hopeful expression, so Sam offered a weak smile. "No problem."

Lorissa's grin was brilliant. "I owe you one."

"Yeah. Remember that."

And in perfect sync, they plunged from the still-warm sand into the oncoming wave.

THE NEXT EVENING, Sam was floating on her back between swells, watching the glorious sun touch its bottom tip on the ocean, that lovely time between day and night, when the birds and stars strained for equal time against a dusky sky. The air was still and hot as the soothingly chilly water lapped over her.

Sam figured she could float out here the rest of the evening and never tire of it.

"*Sam!*"

Damn. Lorissa had found her, and probably just in time for her date. Given the volume of swearing over the roar of the waves, she had precious little time left before her date showed up but she stretched out in the water, trying to swim her doubts away. She didn't often have worries, or so she liked to think, but today she had one big one.

She wished she hadn't agreed to the date. She'd rather be catching the *Bewitched* marathon in her pj's, eating at will. She knew she had the makings for her newest creation—Fritos smashed into cheddar cheese on French bread. She'd melt it over the stove and happily stuff her face—

"Samantha Anne O'Ryan, get your ass out of the water!"

With a sigh, she flipped over and rode a wave in, beaching herself. Flopping onto her back on the hot sand, she shoved her long, blond hair from her eyes and grinned up at a serious-looking Lorissa. "Hey."

Lorissa put her hands on her hips and studied Sam grimly. "I am not amused."

"So I'm running a little late."

"Run late on your *own* night."

"I have ten minutes before he's due to pick me up."

"He's here now."

"Ah, man." Sam sat up, taking the towel Lorissa tossed down into her face. "An obsessive compulsive."

"I've given him a soda. He's sitting at a table."

"But I already closed up."

"Well, I reopened. I'll close again after you're gone. Come on. We'll sneak in the back door, get you into the bathroom to snazzy yourself up."

Samantha glanced down at her efficient, basic black bikini. She was covered in sand and had nasty twin bruises on her thigh and hip, where she'd gotten surprised on her board this morning, tumbling through a full set before managing to get upright. "I look fine."

"Don't even think about it."

"Just kidding. Jeez, lighten up. I'm the one facing Boring Night Out." Sam rose, gently patted Lorissa's cheek. "Honestly, you're just so cute when you're being mom, yelling at me, using my middle name—"

"I'm going to use my middle finger in a minute."

"Yeah, yeah. I'm going."

Taking care not to be seen, they crept in the back kitchen door of Wild Cherries, with Lorissa shoving Sam's head low, beneath the counter.

Once in the bathroom, Sam stepped to the sink and eyed herself. Her mirror didn't lie. Her hair had rioted and she wore no makeup.

"Start fancying yourself up, you look like hell," her supposed best friend said, gesturing to the cold water coming out of the faucet.

"You're going to really owe me," Sam swore, but got to work getting the sand off her body. Then she dipped her head in the sink to rinse the salt out of her hair. "Towel." Blindly, she took it from Lorissa and dried herself.

"And remember," Lorissa instructed, trying to finger-comb Sam's hair. "Don't talk to the press—"

"I remember." She snatched the black cocktail dress hanging on the back of the bathroom stall and started to shimmy into it. The bathroom was small and hot and she wished she was still in the water. "And don't think I haven't noticed that you haven't told me how gorgeous he is."

Lorissa's gaze met hers in the mirror while Sam pulled the little stretchy dress over her bikini. She slipped into the black strappy sandals her surfer buddies would have howled at, knowing she had maybe a thirty-minute window for comfort. After that, Blister City.

"You are *not* going to wear your bathing suit beneath that dress," Lorissa said.

"Well…yeah." Nixing her beloved flip-flops had been smart, because that gave her leverage for this battle.

"The ties from your top show."

"Fine." Lifting her arms up, Sam untied the bikini strap around her neck, and then pulled the top out from beneath the dress. She shoved the still damp bra into her black evening purse. "Just in case."

"In case what—you end up swimming at the Palisades Country Club?"

When she'd found out where they were going, she'd checked it out on the Internet. Fanciest place in town. Probably served jellied fish eggs and drinks she couldn't pronounce. Ugh. Sam touched her hair as she took another look in the mirror. Not great. "Blow-dryer?"

"The thing blew up six months ago and you never replaced it."

"Right. No problem." Twisting up her hair, she searched for something to pin it with.

Lorissa rolled her eyes and pulled the shiny black clip out of her own hair, offering it to Sam. "Makeup."

Sam knew this was not a request. She offered up her face and Lorissa applied blush, mascara and lip gloss. The last item she handed to Sam. "Keep this with you and reapply every once in a while. Please remember that. Now, it's time to get out there and—"

A heavy knock sounded on the bathroom door, accompanied by a low male voice. "Hello?"

In the mirror, Sam raised her brow at Lorissa.

"Uh—hi," he said through the door. "Do you suppose we can get on with this?"

Get on with this? "A real charmer," Sam said beneath her breath.

"I'm sure he's just—"

Another knock. "Hello in there?"

"—in a hurry," Lorissa finished weakly.

"Yeah, well, he'd better be hot," Sam whispered, and with one last deep breath, hauled open the door.

And came face to face with her date.

Or more accurately, her date's broad, wide chest.

"I think he's got the hot covered," Lorissa whispered in her ear.

Good thing she was a fairly tall woman herself, Sam thought vaguely, tilting her head back to catch sight of his face, because the guy had to be six and a half feet tall.

"Oh, good," he said with obvious relief, running his gaze down her own five-foot-ten willowy body. "You're ready." He held out his arm, which she didn't take.

"I don't go out with nameless men," she said.

He looked surprised, as if shocked she had no idea who he was. "Jack Knight," he said in that slightly husky voice.

Okay, not a bad name, she'd give him that. In fact, it sounded vaguely familiar…"Sam O'Ryan."

"Yes, I know. Nice to meet you." He was wearing a tux and a frown, and to her relief, wasn't ugly or fat, but quite…

Actually, Lorissa had put it most aptly. *Hot.* He had dark hair and even darker eyes, a wide, sensual mouth that wasn't smiling at the moment but seemed to have good potential, and a strong jaw covered in a barely there five o'clock shadow, all on top of a long, lean, tough body… Nice combo, she'd admit that.

Not that she was hung up on appearances, but on her run to the bathroom, she'd caught sight of the black Escalade out front. The guy was indeed rich and, as she'd told Lorissa, rich guys usually didn't have much else going for them. So really, she didn't hold out much hope for this one.

But she was committed to tonight. With a last look over her shoulder at Lorissa, she settled her hand on his arm and let him lead her out of the café.

"We probably should have met at a safer location than this," Jack said. As they walked outside into air that was no cooler than the café bathroom had been, he favored his right leg, but she didn't say anything about it because he'd sidetracked her with the "safe" comment. She glanced back at the Wild Cherries sign she'd painted herself five years ago when she'd bought the place from Red.

"It's perfectly safe," she said.

"Now, maybe, but I don't want to drop you off at some isolated hole-in-the-wall later tonight when it's dark. There are no lights out here."

"Watch it," she warned lightly. "I own this hole-in-the-wall, and happen to be quite fond of it, lights or no." She wasn't open at night, so she'd never felt the need to add outdoor lighting.

He glanced at her as he unlocked the passenger door with his remote, but she avoided his gaze until he opened the door and turned his body, blocking her way into his SUV with those long arms and broad shoulders.

Not fond of intimidation, she tipped her head up and slowly cocked a brow, then realized…he wasn't trying to intimidate her at all. Not with his eyes filled with apology and self-deprecation.

"I didn't mean—"

"Forget it." She wasn't willing to fall for a simple sweet look, not when, for all she knew, the man might be full of them.

"No, really." He rubbed the bridge of his nose

and met her sardonic gaze. "Look, obviously, I've made a hell of a first impression."

She felt a smile curve her mouth. "Do you care?"

"Actually, I didn't plan to. But…"

"But…?"

His gaze danced over her features. "I find that I do care." His smile was slow and genuine, and made her tummy flutter. "I want to enjoy this evening with you."

"Why? Because I'm passably pretty?"

"More than passably," he said lightly. "But no, I don't suddenly want to enjoy this just because you turned out to be an extremely pleasant surprise, but because we might as well have fun."

"You mean for two people who didn't want to do this in the first place?"

His smile went to a grin that jump-started her pulse, startling her. "Yeah, something like that."

"Stop that," she said, pointing at his mouth.

"Stop…what?"

"Smiling."

"Why? Do I have something in my teeth?"

He knew he didn't. A guy like this knew exactly how good he looked. "Okay, listen. I'm going to be honest with you right from the get-go."

"Please."

"I have a long, horrible, nasty history with blind dates, and I'd talked myself into lumping you in with the worst of them, but I can't do that when you smile."

The grin only spread. "Really? Well, same goes. I have an idea. Why don't we start over." He stuck out his hand. "Hi, I'm Jack Knight."

"I'm not going to commit to starting over, not yet. You might still turn out to be a blind-date disaster."

"Yeah." He rubbed his jaw. "You might be right."

She climbed into his Escalade. "I usually am."

His soft laugh scraped low in her belly. "Something tells me this is going to be a much more interesting night than I could have imagined."

"Is that good or bad?"

He came around and slid his long body in behind the wheel. He looked at her as he started the engine. "Not sure yet."

"So we'll leave that up in the air as well." With that, Sam put on her seat belt and braced herself for the evening ahead.

But she had a little smile of anticipation on her face.

2

ONCE UPON A TIME, scandal had been Jack's middle name. *Jack Scandal Knight.*

Not that he'd asked for such a rep. Nope, he'd been tried and convicted in the court of the tabloids, without a jury of his peers. But that was in the past.

Tonight, he'd pulled out his tux with a simple goal in mind—get the evening over with as fast and painlessly as possible. No scandal. No surprises. No nothing. Just show up, raise more money for his sister's beloved charity that helped underprivileged kids, then go on his merry way.

Should be easy, given that over the past year he'd become the master of fast and painless, at least as far as public appearances went. The trick was to be visible, but not approachable. Pleasant and professional, but not particularly nice. This talent had been hard-earned, costing him unknown amounts of heartache and grief, but it was a rule he assumed every celebrity eventually learned, one way or another.

All he had to do was arrive at the country club with a date in tow, and his sister would stop pestering him, at least for the evening. Maybe even by some miracle the press would stop hounding him, but he wouldn't hold his breath on that one.

He'd never really been out of the media's spotlight, but that went back to that Jack Scandal Knight thing. He'd have figured no one was interested now that he was no longer in the public eye, but just last week he'd gone to a Dodgers game with a group of friends, where for a few blissful hours he'd eaten hot dogs and had a few beers. After the game, he'd stopped to take a leak and a reporter had come up next to him at the urinal, shoved a camera in his face, blinding him with the flash, and, oh, by the way, could he sign an autograph as well? Jack had looked down at the offered pen, and then farther, to where his hands were busy, and had little choice but to laugh. *Before or after I finish here,* he'd wanted to ask. Five days later, it was splashed all over the rags that he'd been rude and refused to give out autographs.

That was the problem with being a basketball icon known for flying down the court, averaging thirty plus points a game. There was no privacy anywhere. It had been a year since his bum knee had taken him out of the NBA, and his San Diego Eels contract. A *year.*

The paparazzi had been all over him at first, following his every sneeze, apparently not noticing or caring that the difficult decision and subsequent announcement of his retirement had nearly destroyed him.

And *still* they stalked him, given a chance. He didn't know if that was because the Eels hadn't made the championships without him, or because reporters had caught Jack coaching some local kids and thought he might come out of retirement.

Not going to happen. His knee was shot to hell. Two surgeries had left it usable, but not NBA material. And quite honestly, he'd been put through so much by the press, the public and his coaches that he no longer missed playing enough to worry about it.

This charity event tonight, carefully and meticulously planned by his philanthropic sister, would be a nightmare for him. And yet he'd agreed to come because, as asinine as it seemed, just his presence would guarantee money for the kids Heather worked so hard to help. This year, she was raising money for a new rec center, and he wanted to do what he could because he was all for getting those kids into sports and after-school programs, where he'd been volunteering as a coach.

He glanced over at his date as he drove them down the Pacific Coast Highway, the cool air-conditioning blasting out at them. If his presence was going to earn Heather money, then *Sam's* presence was going to earn him kudos from his sister. Heather would find no obvious flaws in Samantha O'Ryan. She had sparkling green eyes and glossy lips, with honey-blond hair piled prettily on top of her head. The long tendrils hanging down made him want to touch. The look was sophisticated and elegant, yet slightly messy at the same time, almost as if she wanted people to know she could lose the image at the drop of a hat and get down and dirty. Incredibly sexy, if you asked him. The rest of her slender body fit into her little black dress, which clung so perfectly to her curves—and very nice curves they were—that he decided he definitely had come out ahead on this deal tonight.

Thank you, Cole. "I appreciate you doing this," he said.

She shrugged and leaned into the AC vent, letting the air blow over her face, which caused a sigh of pleasure to slip out of her that somehow reverberated through him. "A lovely drive and a free dinner. It's no problem."

"And yet you didn't want to come." He smiled, still a little bowled over by the fact she'd had no idea who he was and still didn't. That might have disturbed another man so used to everyone being aware of him, but not Jack. He found it extremely amusing, and oddly refreshing. "You've already alluded to the fact you were worried I was going to be your worst nightmare."

She shot him a wry look. "And what exactly would that be, in your opinion?"

"I don't know…maybe an old guy, with a pot-belly and a bad toupee."

"I don't discriminate against age or shape."

She had her cute nose in the air, and he laughed. "Come on. You were worried about something. Bad breath? Someone too short? Be honest."

"You could still have bad breath, for all I know."

He arched a brow and slanted her another glance. "Not going to admit it could have turned out worse?"

"Hey, the evening is young yet."

"What could go wrong now?" Well, besides being grilled by his sister, and possibly being stalked by the paparazzi guaranteed to be waiting at the front door of the club….

"You could chew with your mouth open," she said and lifted a shoulder. "Or have an extra toe."

He shook his head. "An extra toe?"

"No ugly feet allowed."

"You can't date a guy with ugly feet?"

"Not once I find out about them."

Inside his shoes, he wriggled his toes, thankful

to have only ten, but not sure whether they were ugly. He'd never thought about it. "Tough cookie, aren't you?"

"Yep."

He nodded. He could appreciate tough. He was rather tough himself.

But not with a woman. He'd never kicked a woman out of his bed for ugly feet, that was for damn sure.

"Why did you need a blind date anyway?" She shot him a curious look. "You're not exactly hard on the eyes, or an obvious raving lunatic."

He laughed at the backhanded compliment. "Let's just say I've been out of the dating pool this year, and if I don't show up with a woman tonight, my sister is going to bring out the cavalry."

"Cavalry?"

"Her friends. And their friends. And *their* friends, and so on." He shuddered. "Trust me, it's awful."

"Ah."

Her understanding smile stopped him in his tracks, and he nearly gaped because she had great eyes, and when she smiled like that, they could slay a man at ten miles. "So…" He struggled for something to say, something that would please her and keep that beautiful grin in place. "You own Wild Cherries?"

"Yep."

"Must be nice to be cooked for every day."

Now *she* laughed, the sound light and genuine. "The cook is *moi*. I serve, too, and we've been exceptionally busy, so I guess I should ask myself for a raise. My best friend, Lorissa, helps out, but still, we're usually crazed."

"I'm impressed," he said, loving the sound of her laugh as much as he'd enjoyed her smile. "I usually dial out for my meals. How do you do it all?"

"The café is small, as you saw, and we're only open for the midday and afternoon crowd, so it's not that hard."

"Which leaves you time to…"

"Oh, that's enough about me, I'm not that exciting." She cocked her head at him. "Let's hear about you."

It was a fact of life that women wanted to hear about him, but the thrill of the adoration had worn off years ago. He was the last thing he wanted to think about, much less discuss. "Trust me, I'm really not that exciting, either."

"Somehow I doubt that." She eyed the interior of his SUV. "You live well, you dress well. I'm guessing you also do something for a living pretty darn well."

"Not lately."

She took her eyes off the road and looked at him. "So you're rich and you do nothing?"

"Yeah."

She lifted a shoulder, unimpressed.

That was what he liked about her. Laid-back. Accepting. And for the first time in years, *years*, he found himself relaxing, just letting himself be, because with her there seemed to be no preconceived expectations. She wasn't a groupie, she wasn't trying to leech off his stardom, she wasn't anything but a woman just trying to make the best of a blind date.

He loved that. "I'm retired," he admitted. He waited for her to laugh, or drill him for more answers; in truth, she probably deserved them.

But she just nodded. "Must have been a good run before you called it quits."

"Yeah." A hell of a good run. His team had been infamous for being a tight-knit group and, of course, for their fondness of all things wicked. Sex scandals, gambling scandals, police scandals—name it, and his team had been there, done that. As team captain, Jack had taken the brunt of the fallout. The press had loved the Eels' antics, and they'd loved that Jack had hated them. In fact, after several libel lawsuits that his attorneys had filed and won, they'd joyfully labeled Jack Scandal Knight a prima donna.

He could bike twenty miles a day, bench-press another player and held numerous NBA records.

Yet what did everyone remember him for? A frigging prima donna.

It had gotten so bad that the owners and coaches had clamped down on the team, punishing the players with curfews and brutal practices for even a hint of trouble.

It had been a year since Jack retired, and three years since there'd been any so-called scandal.

And still, even now, after all the hiding out, the press loved to hang him.

For being a prima donna.

That just killed him, truly killed him.

Retired life was definitely simpler than being in the NBA. He could avoid most things media-related—except when his sister needed his name to raise money. And since he'd gotten over the initial shock and letdown of not playing professionally, he'd been happier. Content.

And maybe just a tiny bit bored, he admitted.

He pulled off the Pacific Coast Highway and onto the plush grounds of the country club where tonight's event was taking place. Palm trees lined the half-mile-long driveway which skated past acres of perfectly groomed rolling grass hills overlooking the ocean. The sun was setting on the horizon like a half ball.

His date took one look at the country club as it came into view—the sprawling southwestern-style building set in an impressively lavish garden—and let out a sound that could have been either annoyance or amusement.

"Problem?" he asked, coasting into a parking space and turning to look at her.

"Are you kidding? It's gorgeous. Pompous, but gorgeous." She sounded the same, but her glow was gone, her voice quiet. "I'm sure the food's great." She smiled then, a self-deprecating grin. "Let's just say I'd feel more comfortable in the kitchen than the dining room."

Not expecting such a comment from the woman he'd thought confident and strong-willed, he felt taken aback, and oddly…protective.

But before he could say a word, Sam got out of the car into the warm evening, shutting the door and leaving him to hurry after her. Not easy to do with his knee aching like a son of a bitch—he'd overdone it this week playing with a bunch of hotheaded tenth graders. He came around the car, reaching for her hand to slow her down. "I was thinking maybe we could arrive together," he suggested with a smile.

"Yeah. Okay." She shot him a small smile back. "Sorry."

"Don't be." God, those eyes of hers. They leveled him. "Look…" He turned her to face him. "You seem uncomfortable. How can I change that?"

She stared at him for a second, then smiled. "I think you just did."

He touched her cheek, just one light stroke over her soft skin, a little startled to find himself feeling so…happy. "Good."

"Excuse me, Mr. Knight, could I get an autograph and picture?"

The man with the large camera and press badge had come from nowhere, and Jack steeled himself. "No problem on the autograph," he replied. "But if we could skip the picture—"

A bright flash went off in their faces. Nice. When Jack could see again, the guy was gone. "Sorry," he said to Sam who stood there blinking, and took her hand.

"Who was that?"

"A pest. Come on." A white-carpeted porch led into the club, while the deck above was covered with white awnings, from which hung planters dripping with colorful flowers. At the top of the carpet milled a group of paparazzi, no doubt waiting for the "celebrity" listed on the roster.

Him.

His skin began to itch, an old reaction to bad experiences. He knew he'd have to give them a sound bite once he got inside if he wanted any peace at all. "Stick with me in there."

"What's going on, Jack?"

"In a sec." He pulled her off the walk into the thick grass. Sam gasped and wobbled as her heels sank right in. She lifted a startled gaze to his.

"Piggyback, or in my arms?" he asked.

"What?"

"We're going around the back."

Any woman in the history of his dating life would have stopped cold, stared at him as if he were crazy, and quite possibly even pitched a fit. At the very least, she'd have attracted attention by complaining about the ruining of her heels.

Not this woman.

She pulled the long strap of her little black purse over her head and one shoulder, settling it against her back. Then she tugged up the hem of her dress from mid-thigh to high-thigh. "Piggyback."

He could have kissed her. Instead, he turned his back and bent down a little.

She hopped on. He felt her reach behind, probably checking to make sure she wasn't flashing anyone. "Okay," she said.

He gripped her legs at his sides, adjusting her slightly, and now his hands were each filled with a smooth, tanned thigh. They were firm and lean, and so were her arms, which encircled his neck. "Hold on," he said, enjoying the feel of her toned body plastered to his and the loose tendrils of blond hair clinging to his neck and jaw.

"All set," she said in his ear, her mouth brushing his skin.

A delicious shiver slid down his spine, reminding him that it had been a while since he'd indulged in what was too often thrown at him. In any case, the evening was definitely looking up. Despite the warm night, he began to move through the grass at a fast clip, ignoring the occasional twinge in his knee, concentrating instead on the athletic yet somehow perfectly soft body snugged so intimately to his.

They made it to the line of palm trees undetected, and slipped between them. Now they were far enough off the path so that if people glanced over, they'd merely see a couple walking, but would have no idea of their identity.

Perfect. "You okay back there?"

"Mm-hmm."

The sound vibrated from her chest through his back, and his hands involuntarily tightened on her bare legs. What had started out so innocent had turned unexpectedly and pleasantly...*hot*.

"Are *you* okay?" she asked, her mouth close to his ear, causing more shivers down his spine.

Was he? He was melting, that's what he was, and it had nothing to do with the weather. "Believe me, I've got the good end of the stick on this one," he assured her, extremely aware of his fingers on her smooth, warm flesh.

They reached the building, and Jack moved alongside it. He headed around to the kitchen entrance. Finally he stepped out of the grass and onto concrete. He slowly—reluctantly—let go of her legs so that she could slide to the ground.

And slide she did. He felt every single inch of her, and when he heard her heels hit the deck, he turned. Before he could say a word, the door flung open and Heather stood there in a floor-length sheath of shimmery gold, her long dark auburn hair twisted in some complicated up-do. "You made it," she said with relief. "Quick, inside."

"You leaked this to the press," he accused.

Guilt flashed quickly. "Yes, but only because this time the stalking little bastards are actually going to get the charity's name out there and do some good, so screw them. Plus I made sure they paid the thousand-dollar price tag for the evening. *Each.*" Heather pulled them both into a large, bustling kitchen. There were servers rushing around, filling their trays from bins on the counters.

Heather shut the door behind them and hugged him tight. "You're a sweetie for doing this."

"Just remember that the next time you're pissed off at me for something." Jack pulled free and reached for Sam's hand. "Sam, this is Heather Knight, my sister. Heather, meet Samantha O'Ryan."

"The date I begged you to find." Heather looked Sam over.

His tough, versatile, intriguing, beautiful beach girl looked right back.

"So. Are you real?" Heather asked.

"Excuse me?" Sam blinked. *"Real?"*

"Did he hire you, or are you his real date?"

"Hey," Jack said. "Play nice."

"Hire me?" Sam glanced from one to the other, and then laughed at Jack. "Tell me you are not *that* hard up."

"I am not that hard up." He shot Heather a glare, wanting to strangle her. "She's just insanely bossy. You know, the *much* older sister routine—"

Heather growled at that. "I'm only eleven months older than you, you big lug."

"So you're admitting to being insanely bossy?"

Heather rolled her eyes. "Okay, yes. That part is true."

"You're both crazy," Sam decided.

"Yeah. I'm sorry." Heather actually even looked it. "I'm just a little protective."

"I guess I can understand that." Sam's gaze hooked and held Jack's. "Just as you should understand, I am your brother's date. *Real* date."

Servers continued to hurry past them, but all Jack saw was Sam—the adventurous woman with the contagious smile and amazing eyes in the sexy little black dress. "Definitely a *real* date," he said, not taking his eyes off her.

Sam's grin spread.

And Heather sighed with relief. "Finally, then."

"Just make your money for the kids tonight," Jack said before she could plan their wedding. "Make enough that I don't need the monkey suit again for a while."

"Thanks to a great lineup of auction items, I will. Oh, and I got your donation, by the way. You didn't have to do that, not on top of all the money you've already—"

"Just tell me you have food in there, lots of it, because I'm starving."

"Oh, there's food. Amazing piles of it," Heather assured him. "It's going to get every person in there in a check-writing mood, I hope."

"Good." But Jack's smile suddenly felt a little weak thinking about the evening still ahead, and he braced himself to keep smiling until lockjaw set in.

Sam shot him a curious glance, but didn't say

a word. She just reached out for his hand, which he found himself grabbing on to like a lifeline.

At the moment, it was all he had.

3

SAM LET JACK lead her out of the kitchen and into the main area of the club, which was one huge open room with thick white pillars, gleaming tile floors and sweeping windows overlooking the hills of grass. Beyond them was a breathtaking view of the Pacific Ocean, aflame as the sun set.

Sam tore her eyes from the sight and prepared to be swallowed up by the crowd. She also expected to lose sight of her attractive date because apparently, Jack was a big draw tonight. Already women were staring, most of them with dreamy smiles on their faces, making her feel as if she were back in high school with the captain of the football team at her side like a piece of eye candy.

But even back then, she'd never cared about popularity. She was who she was, and she dated guys who felt the same. Things hadn't changed much. She still didn't care about image, and as a result, her dating circle, small as it was, involved mostly fellow surfers or customers of Wild Cherries. No one had come along and turned her head in a long time.

And yet she felt her head turning now.

Spinning, in fact.

She honestly expected Jack to excuse himself and catch up with her later. She hadn't imagined he'd hold on to her hand with a grip of steel, or that he'd keep looking at her as if he were glad she stood at his side.

They were perfect strangers really, and yet… she held on to him as well, and felt a thrill go through her when he looked at her as if she were the most beautiful woman in the room.

The north corner was set up for dining, with rows of tables covered in white linens and china. In the south corner a band was playing, while people milled, conversed and danced.

Everyone was dressed to the hilt, sedate and professional in their partying. Sam and Jack passed a group of women in shimmery gowns, each with a man in a tux on her arm. Most stopped talking, shooting Jack more than a passing glance.

Interesting.

"Don't look directly at them," Jack murmured in her ear, still holding tight to her hand. "Smile, but keep your feet moving."

"I think they want to talk to you…"

"Like I said, keep moving." Obviously an expert at working a crowd, he weaved and dodged like a pro quarterback even when people turned toward him and tried to head him off at the pass. He kept smiling and nodding his head, but with admirable skill, avoided being detained by anyone with a camera.

"Impressive," she murmured, and then began to catch snippets of conversation going on around them.

"My God, it's him."

"Mmm, looking hot as ever, too."

"The Eels never recovered after he left. He shouldn't have left."

That one had Jack's jaw tightening, and Sam felt an odd surge of protectiveness for the man. How dare these people act as if he couldn't hear them.

"Who cares why he really quit. I just miss seeing his buns in basketball shorts."

"Take a shower, Marge."

The last was probably a disgusted husband, but Sam tripped over her heels as it hit her. *Jack Scandal Knight.* She was Jack Scandal Knight's blind date. My God, how had she not realized? He had athlete written all over him—from the long, hard, rangy length of him, to the rigid yet easy control in every movement he made.

He wasn't the quarterback she'd just imagined, but a basketball star.

He caught her. "You okay?"

She looked up into his startlingly handsome face and nodded. Why hadn't he told her? What was it he'd said...? He'd *retired*. She supposed it had been easier to define it that way rather than as millions of others did—going out as a legend in his own time.

She imagined his reticence was because everywhere he went, people fawned over him, or just talked about him, as they were doing now, as if he wasn't in the room.

This was crazy. Jack Scandal Knight, holding her hand, pulling her along.

"Jack, tell us when you're coming back to the game."

Jack sighed and squeezed her hand. "Sorry, but I have to say something or they'll never leave us alone." He turned to the group of reporters on their right. Ten mikes were immediately shoved in his face. Flashes went off. "I had a great run," he said. "I loved every minute of it, but I'm not coming back to the game. I'm here to support this evening's charity, which gives money and attention to underprivileged kids." He smiled, held still for another moment for pictures, then backed away.

Sam moved with him, wondering how his life had changed since he'd stopped playing. Given the expert weave and bob he was executing, it hadn't changed much. He didn't want the press around him, he didn't want any attention at all. There was something…cute about that.

If one could call a six-foot-six, tough-as-nails, hard-as-rock man cute.

In the middle of the large room now, he took a deep breath, and when a group of men came up to him, not reporters, but guests, Jack shook their hands warmly.

"How's retirement?" one asked. "Great?"

"How could it not be?" Jack answered. "And how are you all doing tonight?"

Everyone murmured their answer, then someone said to Jack, "What are you doing with yourself these days?"

"Keeping busy, that's for sure. Who's actually played golf here? Is it any good?"

It went on like that for a few minutes, with Jack dodging and deflecting. She could see how private he was, and she wondered how a man like that dealt with such public pressure.

After a few minutes, Jack excused them and led her away. They passed a waiter holding a large tray of champagne. "Thank God." He let go of her hand to grab two flutes, one of which he handed to her. Then he let out a long sigh and clinked his glass lightly against hers. "To the best evening we can make out of this."

"Well, we've done pretty good so far."

"Yeah." A genuine smile touched his lips. "We sure have. And I think most of the press actually left after their photo op. Thanks for being so patient."

Around them, the crowd tightened, closing in a little, and she was forced into him. "Sorry," she murmured, backing away to give him some room, only to bump into a couple behind her, nearly spilling her drink.

"Come here," Jack said softly, sliding his free hand down the length of her arm, entwining his fingers through hers. Shifting their connected hands to the small of her back, he gently urged her forward and once again into him.

Now her hips were cradled rather intimately with his, her breasts brushing his chest. The connection came on like a strong jolt, and her gaze flew up to his.

Jack felt it, too; she could see the heat in the dark depths of his eyes reflected back at her. "So maybe," he murmured, "the toast should be to the rest of the evening."

"Yes…" Dipping her head, she took a sip from her flute to cover her confusion at her unusually strong reaction to him, but then caught a movement over his shoulder. "Mob closing in at two o'clock."

He swore, tossed his champagne down his

throat and ditched the glass on a different waiter's empty tray before getting them on the move again.

They headed toward the band, who'd struck up a Seventies disco beat. The lights went down and at least ten disco balls lowered from the ceiling swirling and sending flashes of light into every corner.

"Join us for disco hour," the band leader said into his microphone. "And at eight o'clock, we'll move into the Eighties."

The crowd perked up, and many moved toward the dance floor.

Sam looked at the colored lights, at the people starting to move to the beat, and nerves leaped into her throat. Surely Jack wouldn't expect her to dance in these ridiculous heels and tight dress...

He stopped at the edge of the dance floor, thank God. They could just watch—

"Okay, I think it's safe here," he said. "Quick, gaze into my eyes like I'm the only man you see. Maybe that'll keep everyone away."

She laughed, but dutifully looked into his eyes. "Like you're the only man I see? And how does one give that kind of a look?"

He blinked, then laughed, too. "Actually, I haven't a clue."

"Uh-oh." She winced. "Sorry to tell you, there

are three men in cheap suits holding cameras, making their move."

"Damn." Grabbing her hands, Jack pulled her onto the dance floor, then glanced back at the photographers stymied at the side of the room. Heather swiftly moved in and shifted them out of sight, winking at Jack over her shoulder.

Jack smiled down at Sam. "Better."

They were surrounded by couples gyrating to the music. "Unless you know something else we can do out here," she said, "we actually have to dance." She could surf wave after wave, she could stand on the counter of her café and sing at the top of her lungs when the mood struck her, but swaying in time to the music was hard. She had no rhythm.

With a smoothness that startled her, Jack slid one arm around her waist, took her free hand in his and pulled her toward him. "Dancing works for me."

"Wait—" The air rushed out of her when she came up against his big, warm, hard body. He felt good, and that was before he began to sway in perfect time to the music. She stared at him. "You know how to do this?"

In the dark, his smile flashed white. "Why the surprise?"

Because athletes, famous ones, were usually

good at only one thing—their sport. But he had rhythm, good rhythm, and moves that made her mind wander into areas she hadn't expected to go this evening.

"What's the matter?" he asked when she stood there in his arms, stiff and unmoving.

What was the matter? Nothing, except that she felt like an idiot. For all her wild days in her crazy youth, she'd never really gotten comfortable with this elementary skill. She'd never wanted to. But she had a gorgeous man holding her in his arms, his entire attention focused on her as they tried to forget the world around them, and she really did want to help him forget. In any other way except this.

He dipped his head down a little, ran his jaw over hers. "Sam?"

She could sense the firmness of his body. She could even feel his heart beating, strong and steady, and she stared up at him, one arm around his neck, her other hand entangled in his, absorbing the strength of his fingers at the small of her back, the pressure of his hips swaying gently against hers. Her body reacted, hormones revved, bones melted…

How did a man who palmed a basketball for a living get to be so sensual?

"Sam? You still with me?"

"It's just that dancing seems so…clichéd."

"Clichéd," he repeated. "Dancing on a dance floor is clichéd?"

"Yes. I'm sure we could find something else to do." *Anything*…

"Like…?"

"Um, like…" She searched her brain, feeling a little disoriented by the pulsating lights from the disco balls. "I don't know. *You* think of something."

"No, I think *you'd* better." His eyes were deep and dark, his hands gentle on her, and also, whether he intended it not, unbearably erotic. "Because suddenly, with you looking at me like that, I can't seem to think of anything appropriate."

Well, neither could she! In fact, a bunch of inappropriate thoughts kept bouncing through her head, and her body slid even closer to his.

Now what? She knew what her body would like, and her hand glided over his chest, her fingers curling into him.

"Sam—"

The lights went down even more, so that all they could see were the silhouette of the people dancing around them. Perfect camouflage. Sliding her hands into the hair at the nape of Jack's neck, she tugged his head down closer, and planted her lips on his.

The sexy little surprised murmur he made echoed through her, tingling her nerve endings, over-sensitizing them, and she wound her arms tighter around his neck as her eyes drifted shut.

Technically, she should have shut her eyes before then, but she'd waited to make sure he was okay with the direction in which she'd just taken the evening.

Given the way he slanted his head for a better angle, while hauling her up against him even closer, he was good with the new direction— quite good.

Kissing a man for the first time was always an experience, an adventure—not unlike the story of Goldilocks. Would he use too much tongue, not enough tongue or just the right amount? But Jack Scandal Knight kissed *juuuusssst* right.

And he didn't pull away, not even when they were both breathless. He had one hand on her hip, the other on her spine, fingers spread wide, and when she slid her hands down to his shoulders, sinking into his tough, hard muscle, he let out another groan, low in his throat.

At the sound, something came over her on that dark dance floor. Lust, yes, but this felt different. It gripped her and held on like a bulldog; she couldn't bear to back away, not even to come up for air. She simply dragged her mouth over his jaw, and let out a little whimper when he did the same. Her fingers tightened on his hair, tugging just a little, while her hips danced to his, and he let out another low groan.

"Not fair," he managed.

"Why?"

"I'm not going to be able to walk off this dance floor for a while."

Suddenly, she didn't want to move, either, and she arched against him, nearly seeing double when his thigh rubbed against hers.

With a glance around, making sure that no one was paying them any attention, he cupped her face. "Sam...what are you doing to me?"

Hopefully driving him half as wild as he was driving her. Avoiding a dance had become the last thing on her mind. "I should mention..." She sank her teeth into his lobe, thrilling to the sound that dragged from him. "It's been a little too long for me. I'm liking this way too much."

"Don't tell me that." One hand skimmed up her back, the other was on her hip. His thumb glided over her belly, upward, stroking, tracing her last rib, barely skimmed over the very bottom curve of her breast.

All the while, his gaze held hers, conveying hunger, passion, desire...more heady than the champagne she'd sipped. She let out a shuddery breath, her bones long dissolved away.

Then he took another sweep with his thumb,

not quite touching her nipple, and she had to concentrate on breathing.

"Sam." His voice was low, hoarse.

Sinking her fingers into his hair again, she brought his mouth back to hers, and their moans commingled, becoming a part of the crazy, wild kiss.

Then the song ended, and the lights came up slightly as the band leader started talking about their next set.

Jack's eyes were sleepy and very sexy when they opened on Sam's. "What else will you do to keep from dancing?"

"Um…that was about it." At least that she was willing to admit.

His eyes flitted down to the front of her dress, where her hard-as-rock nipples were pouting against the black material, begging for more attention, and he let out a low groan that pulled at them even more.

It was getting crowded, with people dancing in earnest now the music had started again. Everyone looked as if they knew exactly what they were doing as they gyrated and swayed on the floor.

Oh boy. Sam tugged on Jack's hair again and put her mouth back on his. With a soft, silky laugh, he obliged her for a long moment, until finally, dizzy, dazed with lust, she lifted her head for air.

"Are you really going to let me keep kissing you to avoid dancing?"

He was breathing heavily, too. "Oh, yeah."

4

SAM BLEW OUT a breath and looked at Jack. "Okay, truth," she told him. "I don't dance. In fact, I stink at it."

"But we were just doing it."

"That was slow dancing. And you did all the work."

He couldn't take his eyes off the woman who'd just rocked his world with a flash of both heaven and hell in one kiss—heaven, because she'd been soft and delicious; hell, because he suspected that was all he was going to get. How could a woman so self-possessed, so naturally sensual, *not* dance? "Come on, really?"

"Really."

He thought about that while the feel of her body against his sank into his brain. Her nipples were still hard, her arms tight around his neck, and she wasn't the only one affected. He wanted her with a surprising hunger. But when he had her—please God, he'd have her—it would be in a much more private location than this.

The next best thing to that would be another nice, long slow dance where she could writhe and arch against him, and he'd close his eyes and inhale her. But this song wasn't slow. "I'll help you."

"Jack—"

"Come on," he coaxed, moving to the beat. "It's not that difficult. First, you feel. Feel me, feel the music—hey, you have to at least try. Hang on, this song is ending— Oh, you lucked out," he said as the band ended the fast upbeat number and launched into an achingly slow love song. He pulled her just a little bit closer. "Mmmm, nice." His lips brushed against her ear, and suddenly it took all the willpower he had not to start kissing her again. "Better," he whispered, when she softened against him.

After a few moments, she let out a long, slightly shaky sigh. Her fingers curled into the fabric of his shirt as an entirely different kind of tension gripped them. Swaying with him, eyes closed, he felt her smile against his shirt.

"I can't believe I'm liking this evening," she said.

"Me, too."

"A small part of me really was banking on you having that potbelly or bad breath, something awful."

"Sorry to disappoint you." He pulled back and

looked into her eyes. "I'm also sorry about the whole sneaking in here thing."

"Don't be." She shot him a wry smile. "Or then I'd have to be sorry about kissing you to avoid dancing."

"You didn't kiss me just to avoid dancing."

She stared at him. "No," she finally whispered. "I didn't."

"And you didn't let me touch you just to avoid dancing, either."

Another slow shake of her head. "No. I wanted both."

His gaze dropped to her mouth. Her fingers played at the back of his neck, urging him closer, then closer still. It was all the encouragement he needed, and he dipped his head and kissed her. It sent hot licks of desire skittering down his spine. Locked in her arms, mouth against mouth, it was somehow easy to forget the press, the people, his sister, everything, lost as he was in the taste and feel of her.

She pulled away first, looking as shell-shocked as him. They made a couple of more turns on the dance floor, silent. Heather was out there with her date, and she waved at them.

"Did I mention I'm sorry about her, too?" Jack asked.

"Because she's overprotective? I think it's sweet."

"She's worried someone's going to take advantage of me, if you can imagine that happening."

"Only if you were willing," Sam said.

He laughed. "Willing... Do you want to take advantage of me, Sam?"

Oh, yeah, Sam did want to do just that. Now, please. But the truth was, she didn't know him well enough to sleep with him yet. "I haven't decided," she said as honestly as she could.

Eyes still on hers, his smile became a little subdued and he nodded slowly. "I wouldn't want to rush that decision."

Her body tightened, yearned. "Thank you," she said so politely he grinned broadly. The music changed again, and so did Jack's tempo. Faster and faster, he whirled her around the floor with dizzying speed.

"Where did you learn to do that?" she asked breathlessly when the song ended.

"My sister. In high school, if she couldn't get a date, she made me be her partner."

"*Made* you?"

"She spied on me for ammo, which she'd detail in a diary she kept locked up to use as blackmail when necessary. And, believe me, she found it necessary a lot. God, she loved holding stuff over my head."

"That sounds…" Sam searched for a word. "Horrible."

"Spoken like a woman who has no siblings?" he guessed.

"Not a one."

"How about your parents? Didn't you ever dance with them?"

She hesitated, never knowing what to say. She hated pity, and talking about her past always evoked that in others. Luckily, another couple bumped into them. The woman dripped diamonds and the man with her wore a dopey, infatuated grin. "Jack Knight," he said reverently. "Miss you, man."

"Thanks," Jack said.

"I must have an autograph for my son," the woman said. "After the dance?"

"No problem."

"I noticed you're not entirely a social pariah," Sam said when they were alone again—or as alone as they could get on a crowded dance floor.

"Nah, it's only the people who want something that bug me."

"That couple wanted something. Your autograph."

"Yeah, but an autograph, that's easy to give. It's when they want a piece of your soul that you've got to watch out. So," he said lightly, changing the subject on her like a champ. "Your parents. They never twirled you around the kitchen floor?"

Her father had been a professor at Pepperdine University, her mother an administrator in the offices there. They'd loved her, but they'd been incredibly devoted to their work, disciplined to long hours, with little time off for such things as dancing in the kitchen. "No twirling around the floor for us, I'm afraid."

"I think everyone should have memories of dancing in their pj's, slipping in their socks on the linoleum with their family."

"Mine weren't the dancing kind."

His easy smile faded. "Past tense?"

"They're both gone now. They have been for a long time."

People never knew what to say when she said that, and subsequently did one of two things—said they were sorry, or awkwardly changed the subject.

Jack did neither. "That's incredibly unfair."

"Yeah."

The song ended. People began to talk. Many looked their way. A few with cameras started walking toward them.

"Oh boy," Jack said.

A surge of protectiveness rose within Sam,

which was silly. The guy could take care of himself, and yet she pointed to the long row of tables set up against one wall, piled with lavish amounts of food. Her stomach growled, reminding her she hadn't eaten since breakfast. "Food. People won't want to stare at you if you're eating. Unless…you don't by any chance eat with your mouth open…?"

He laughed. "Not usually."

"Okay, then."

They each took a plate. She eyed the salads and, saving herself for the big guns up ahead, spooned a small amount of fruit salad onto her plate.

"Tell me you're going to eat more than that."

"Oh, I'm going to eat *much* more." Farther down, she stabbed a nice sized steak, then helped herself to a roll and a huge heap of potatoes.

"Good." He piled his plate high, as well. "I might have had to throw you to the press as bait if you'd stuck with only fruit."

They walked to the least crowded table, which so far held only two women and a man, all three at least seventy years old. The women sipped their drinks and the man sandwiched between them had a very contented look on his face as he ate.

Jack gave them an easy smile. "Hello."

The man returned a full-fledged grin. "I'd call

you one lucky SOB for escorting a woman as beautiful as you've got there…" His voice was craggy, as if he'd been smoking for fifty-plus years. "But tonight *I'm* the lucky SOB because I've got two beautiful dates."

Jack laughed as he held Sam's chair out for her. When he sat, he lifted his water glass to the man. "To having beautiful women at our side."

"I'll drink to that," the man said.

They began to eat. Sam found herself watching Jack. When he caught her at it, he smiled. "What?"

He had such a graceful, smooth way of moving when he danced, ate…everything. It made looking at him very easy on the eyes. "What else do you like besides a woman who eats more than a carrot stick?" she asked softly.

When he simply looked at her, she let out a little laugh. "I was…just wondering."

He set down his fork. Reached for her hand. "I like a woman who can come out of the waves and get ready for a date in two minutes."

"Saw that, did you?"

"Yeah." He stroked a thumb over her palm. "I like a woman who can go with the flow, risking the wet grass to help me out without worrying about her shoes. I like a woman who doesn't take down a guy's sister even when she's interfering and deserves it. And I really like a woman willing to try new things, like dancing in front of several hundred people when she hates dancing."

"Well, I didn't risk the grass, you carried me." And she'd loved it, his easy strength, the feel of his hands on her. She took a bite of mashed potatoes that melted in her mouth. "And as for the dancing, you did all the work. I've never felt comfortable dancing."

"You felt comfortable to me."

Yeah, in hindsight, being in his arms had been pretty damn comfortable. Hot, too.

And exciting, very exciting.

He scooped up some fancy-looking noodle salad onto his fork and held it up to her lips.

"Something else new to try this evening?" she murmured, and took the bite into her mouth.

"Nah." His voice was low and husky, his gaze glued to her mouth. "I just love watching you eat."

AFTER DINNER came the auction.

Jack eyed the long roster of prizes at his place setting, knowing that he was coming up on the list. He and Sam had watched the proceedings so far, eating their self-made ice-cream sundaes from the dessert bar. Someone had just won on a two-day trip to Santa Barbara, and then a ski package to Big Bear. Each time the bidding ended, Sam turned to him, her eyes bright with excitement, her hand on his arm, grinning.

"So much money for Heather's charity!" she'd said after one huge round. "Unbelievable."

What was unbelievable was tonight. He'd expected to be bored, but that had been the last thing on his mind... "Sam."

She was watching Heather run the auction. "I like her. I mean, she's pushy but I've been known to be pushy, too, so—"

"*Sam.*"

Laughing, she put down her spoon, licked her lips and turned to him. "Hmm?"

Her eyes were shining, her hair still in that sexy, messy bun that made him want to pull it out and run the strands through his fingers. Unable to help himself, he reached out and ran a finger over her full lower lip, where she'd missed a spot of ice cream.

He brought his finger up to his mouth and sucked on it.

Her eyes darkened and her mouth fell open just a little, as if she was suddenly having trouble breathing.

He certainly was. "I'm up next."

She stared at his mouth. "What?"

"The auction. I donated something, and it's about to come up on the list."

"How sweet. What did you donate?"

"Myself."

Just as he said this, Heather's voice came over the loud speaker. "And now for the finale…a series of private two-hour basketball lessons from one of the greatest players of our time—Jack Knight. We'll start the bidding at two hundred dollars."

Still turned toward him, Sam raised her eyebrows slightly, the only sign she'd heard and digested Heather's words.

"Two fifty," Heather said, acknowledging the man at one of the front tables who had gestured.

Sam grabbed her bidder's paddle. She hadn't bid all evening, and Jack had already given a healthy check, so he hadn't, either.

But now, with her eyes still locked on his, Sam lifted the paddle.

"Two seventy-five," she said.

From her platform, Heather grinned. "I've got two seventy-five, do I hear three hundred?"

"Three hundred," called a man in the back.

Sam's wrist flexed as she tried to lift her paddle again, but Jack laughed and held it down. "Stop," he said.

She stuck out her tongue at him, and he had the insane urge to suck it into his mouth.

"Three fifty," she called out.

The bidding got crazy after that, and Jack gave up holding Sam back, but he worried as he watched her go at it with such glee. "Sam—"

"We're at seven fifty," Heather said excitedly. "Going once—"

"Eight hundred," Sam called out.

"Eight hundred," Heather called, looking impressed. "Going once, twice…" She slammed down her gavel. "Sold, to the lady in black with the big smile on her face."

Jack laughed, he couldn't help it. Sam was grinning. "You're crazy."

"Probably."

"You didn't have to do that."

"Don't worry, Jack," she said softly. "I never do anything I don't want to do."

"Is that right?" He stroked a wayward tendril of hair from her eye, ran his finger down her jaw. "What would you like to do now?"

"Are we finished here?"

"I don't know about you, but I am."

"Then let's hit it." She stood up, then reached for his hand.

They found Heather, harried but happy with the money she'd collected so far. Sam settled up for her purchase and got her coupon for the lessons.

Heather hugged Jack hard. "Thanks for doing this. I know I owe you."

He looked at Sam, thinking about what he'd gotten out of the evening. "Consider us even."

"It wasn't so bad, right?" Heather asked. "No scandals."

"Were you expecting one?" Sam asked.

"No, but with Jack, the press will make one up if they have to. They love to hang him." Heather kissed his cheek, and then Sam's. "'Night, guys."

"'Night." Jack opened the back door and put a hand low on Sam's spine to guide her out.

"Oh. Uh, I just remembered…" Heather's voice trailed off.

Jack sighed and turned back to see Heather standing there, hands clasped. "I know better than to stop and ask *what* you just remembered."

"One last little favor…"

"What?"

"A carnival for the kids," Heather said. "Next weekend. We're short of volunteers. It'd only be for a few hours, the two of you could do it together. It'll be fun, I promise."

Jack sighed.

"Free food…"

Sam looked up at him expectantly. "I like free food."

He had to let out a laugh. "You did hear the 'two of you' part, right?" he asked. "Which means, you're involved now whether you like it or not."

"I wouldn't mind."

"For the children," Heather said sweetly. "It's all about the kids, Jack."

"Which booth?" he asked. "Because you're not telling me something, I can tell."

"Well, it's a simple one, really. Very easy to run. You'll have no problem with it at all. And the children just love it—"

"Which booth, Heather?"

His sister rolled her eyes. "The dunking booth."

Jack raised his eyebrows at Sam. "See?"

"I don't have a problem with a dunking booth," Sam said. "I like water."

Both women grinned and turned to face Jack, but it was Sam's promising smile that grabbed him, and he groaned because he knew.

He was a goner.

5

THEY MADE a late-night stop at McDonald's for sodas—both aware they were just trying to make the evening last—and Sam couldn't get over how much she laughed as they sat at that little table in the empty fast-food place. In fact, she couldn't believe the entire evening—everything about it and her date had made her smile.

But the smile faded as they walked back to the SUV. The night was quickly coming to an end, and now she needed an answer to the eternal question.

To kiss or not to kiss.

Actually, the question was moot now, wasn't it? She'd already gone that far, with an ease that shocked her. Tonight had been so much more than she'd bargained for, and she felt the need to retreat and think.

So as they got into his car and drove toward the café, she made the decision not to tell Jack she lived above it, mostly because she wouldn't be able to resist him if he asked to come in.

On the highway, Jack reached out and took her hand. His expression sent little shivers of pleasure down her spine. She knew he wanted more than a kiss.

And so did she.

But wanting more and getting it were two separate things. Nope, she needed to sleep on this one, which meant neither of them were going to get what they wanted, not tonight.

THE MOON hung above the waves, making the frothing white water glow as they pulled into the café's parking lot.

Jack had felt Sam's retreat, and he turned to her. "You okay?"

She smiled at him, though it didn't quite make it to her eyes. "Sure."

"Sam."

"I'm just thinking." She put her hand on his arm, making him feel better. "I get quiet when I think. Thanks for tonight. It was nice."

"Yeah, it was." He turned off the engine and walked around to her side of the SUV.

"'Night," she said, poised for flight.

"At least let me walk you to your car."

"That's okay, I'm going to go inside for a minute. I've got stuff to do."

Nodding, he studied her face by moonlight, or

what he could see of it since she wouldn't look directly at him, and wondered what had happened to scare her off. "You work late out here a lot?"

"Sometimes." Again she looked a little distant, as if in her mind she were already inside the café working. "I'll be safe, don't worry." With another flash of a half smile, she turned away.

He snagged her wrist in a light hold, ran his thumb over her pulse. "Sam—"

"I've got to go, Jack." But in a surprising move, considering she'd already dismissed him, she leaned into him and gave him a quick kiss.

The press of her soft mouth on his was welcome, but all too quickly she pulled away and walked off into the night.

Despite her sudden silence, and how quickly she appeared to want to get rid of him, he stood there for a moment watching her.

She didn't go into the café.

She didn't get into her car.

But she did disappear over the bluff beside the café.

Curious, he followed her, and stopped dead at the top of the rise. Her high-heeled sandals lay discarded at his feet. Lifting his head, his eyes searched the night. There she was, silhouetted at the water's edge. Before he could so much as move, she raised her hands behind her and unzipped her dress.

Then let it fall.

Oh, man.

The moonlight bathed her body as she kicked free of the dress pooled at her ankles. Wearing only what looked like black panties, she straightened. The thin moonlight streamed over her body, lighting up her shoulders and her slim back.

Still not turning to face him, she stepped into the water a few feet, and when a wave came in, she dived into it and vanished.

Unable to believe his eyes, he stood there in frozen shock for a beat, and then when she didn't surface, started running down the dune toward the beach. He scanned the waves but couldn't see her. "Sam!"

He had kicked off his shoes, shucked his jacket, and had his fingers on the zipper of his pants when her wet blond head resurfaced, way out there now, past the next set of waves.

She dived again.

She was bodysurfing.

That had him relaxing, but only marginally. Now that he was no longer afraid for her, something else had taken him by the throat.

The way she looked, more than half-naked and wet by moonlight.

His fingers started working again, and he

pushed his pants down and peeled off his socks. He tossed his shirt the way of his tux jacket.

And plunged in.

The shock of the cold water took his breath for a moment, but it was exhilarating, too, and he began swimming. When the first set of waves came upon him, he took a deep breath and dived beneath them, feeling them crash over him with thunderous pressure.

He surfaced, grabbed another breath and ducked under the next wave, letting the momentum take him through.

With the black sky above him and the blacker sea swirling beneath him, it was almost a surreal experience, with no clear definition of what was up and what was down.

Feeling awe-inspired for no obvious reason, he dived through the final set of waves and surfaced next to Sam.

With a gasp she turned her head and blinked at him, her body covered up to her shoulders with the dark, fathomless, turbulent water. "Jack. You scared me to death."

"What did you think I was, a shark?"

A hint of a smile curved her mouth. "I would have been less surprised."

"You didn't think I could swim?"

"I thought you were long gone."

"You've never had a guy want to walk you to your door before, or make sure you were truly safe before he took off?"

Instead of answering, she let the next swell take her, and then she disappeared under a wave. But she must have been thinking about what he'd said because when she swam back to him, she tossed back her blond hair and said, "I've been on my own for a long, long time."

He had no idea why that both appealed to him and tugged at him. Floating a little closer, he looked into her eyes. "You're not alone right now."

"Maybe I want to be."

"Really?"

She stared at him, then let out a sighing laugh. "No." She took the next swell, and the next, then after a while came to him. "You still here?"

Jack touched her face. "Still here. Don't people stick around for you, Sam?"

"Some."

"Do you have any family?"

"I have an uncle. And I consider Lorissa my family, too."

His heart softened some more. As much as his sister drove him crazy, as much as his parents bossed and nudged and invaded and tried to run his life, he loved them all and couldn't imagine being without them. "How old were you when you lost your parents?"

"Hey, here comes a good one, you going to take it?" She made a sound of annoyance when the wave passed them, lifting them high for a long beat in time, then dropping them back down.

The amazing pull of the tide, the way of the earth.

"Don't blow another one," she said.

So he didn't. He took the next swell and rode it in, finding himself grinning in the black night as he swam back out to her. "I don't think anything beats this, bodysurfing at midnight."

"No, nothing does." She swam a little closer, treading water. "I was fourteen," she said quietly. "They died in a car wreck."

He smiled faded. "God. What did you do?"

She lifted a shoulder. "I was all right. I went to my uncle Red's. And I had lots of friends so I was never really alone. I'm taking this one."

And she vanished on the next breaker, diving into it, flashing him a quick glimpse of her barely covered gorgeous ass.

When she came back, grinning from ear to ear, he found himself reaching for her, putting his hands on her hips, keeping them both afloat with his legs. The water swirled around her shoulders. "Was your uncle good to you?"

"As good as he knew how to be." Kicking free,

she retreated and took the next wave. When she showed up again, she drifted close, but not close enough to touch.

"Sam...I can't even imagine."

Again, she lifted a bare, glistening shoulder. "I had it okay. Got to go through high school without anyone telling me what I could or couldn't do, or that I was being stupid, or that I wasn't trying hard enough..."

"I had a family," he said quietly. "And no one ever told me any of that."

"No? Then you're lucky, too."

Comparing her life to his boggled his mind. "Your parents left you enough money to get by?"

"Some, but their estate was sued, and lost."

His heart broke for her.

She splashed him. "Get that pity off of your face and take the next swell, or I will."

"That's not pity on my face, it's empathy." He tugged her close. "Can't you let anyone be sensitive to what you've been through?"

She thought about that. "No."

Well, she was going to start, he decided. She was squirming a little, probably trying to calculate how to outswim him and vanish. Couldn't have that. And not just because he had her bare breasts against his chest.

But she slipped out of his arms and beneath the

surface of the water, and came up five feet away. She took the next wave and the next. When she finally returned, he asked, "Is bodysurfing naked by moonlight a hobby?"

"I'm not naked, I'm wearing my bikini bottoms."

"Ah. Well then…do you always go on dates in your bikini bottoms?"

"I usually wear my top, too, but Lorissa made me take it off because apparently it ruined the line of the dress."

He silently blessed Lorissa.

"And if I'd known you were going to spy on me here tonight, I'd have pulled it out of my purse and put it back on before I got in the water."

"You…have your bathing suit in your purse."

"When it's not on me, yes. I spend a lot of time in the water."

"Bodysurfing in the middle of the night."

"And in the early mornings, and swimming in the afternoons when I can fit it in. Jack, why are you here?"

"Maybe I like the water, too." He'd never really cared one way or another, but Sam had changed his mind tonight.

"You should go home."

"Why?" He drifted toward her. "Am I getting too close?"

She splashed him again, and this time she wasn't smiling.

Look at that, he thought with some amusement, the surfer girl has a temper. "Okay, you're right."

"About…"

"I should open up to you before making you open up to me."

"I didn't say that."

"No, but you should have. Want to hear a deep dark secret?"

"Jack—"

"I don't miss basketball. Everyone thinks I do, but I don't. Not anymore."

"You really don't?"

"I miss playing but I don't miss being a celebrity."

"You're still a celebrity."

"But I don't want to be."

She stared at him for a long time, then laughed. "That I believe."

"Now you."

"Now me what?"

"Now you tell me a secret about you."

Another wave passed and neither of them took it. "I'm tired," she said. "I'm going in."

"Liar," he chided softly.

She was already a few strokes into her swim back but she stopped and looked at him over her shoulder. "Maybe my secret is worse than yours."

"Tell me."

"I'm…" She rolled her eyes. "You might have already guessed."

"Say it anyway."

"I'm a commitmentphobe. Okay?"

"Very okay." He swam toward her. "Since we share in that trait."

"You're an unusual man, Jack Knight."

"Thank you. I think." They started swimming toward shore again, riding a few big swells in, rolling into each other, laughing. By the time they hit the sand they were entangled in each other's arms.

The water retreated, and Jack looked down at the half-naked woman against him. Her body was long and lean, chilled and yet somehow warm and soft, so wonderfully soft. Her bare breasts were perfect handfuls—or perfect mouthfuls—and his mouth watered at the thought.

Their bodies brushed together, her nipples hardening against his pecs, making him want to die of pleasure. Her legs entwined with his, and he looked down at her glorious body, wet and radiant beneath the night. His laughter had long ago faded, replaced by a burst of white-hot, gut-wrenching lust.

A look that was mirrored in Sam's eyes, thank God.

"I meant what I said," he murmured hoarsely, keeping his eyes on hers. "I'm no more into promises than you are. But you should know, I find you so attractive and sexy, I can hardly breathe when I look at you."

She lifted her hands and slid her fingers into his hair. "So it's all surface attraction only, just skin-deep. Right?"

Surface attraction, skin-deep. Yeah, right up his alley. But somehow, this time, with this woman, the description seemed a little...cold. "Sam—"

"Skin-deep is all I do, Jack. Know that right now. I'm not being coy or playing a game. It's the way I am."

"Yeah." How many times had he said the same thing? He looked down at her body interlocked with his and felt the ball of fire in his gut stoke into flame. Shifting a hand up her hip and over her belly, his thumb skimmed her breast.

Her breath hitched. Goose bumps rose over her skin. He wanted to haul her close and smooth each one away, but she shifted out of his arms.

"Hey, even a beach bum like me doesn't do skin-deep on the first date." Bending, she scooped up her discarded dress. Stepping into it, she pulled it up, covering that body he knew he'd be dreaming about tonight. She struggled with the zipper.

With a sigh and a groan for the quick flash of pain in his knee, he rose to his feet and came up behind her. Gently, he set her hands aside and zipped her wet, beautiful skin into the dress.

She turned to face him and smiled, her earlier wariness gone. "Thanks."

"My pleasure."

She looked down at his feet.

"Ten toes, notice," he pointed out.

"I can see that." She smiled. "And they're not ugly."

"I'm glad you approve."

"Tonight really *was* nice, Jack."

She seemed so surprised. He cupped her face, stepped closer. "I'm glad for that, too."

"I guess I didn't expect it to be."

"Me neither," he said quite honestly.

"Yeah..." She took a step backwards, then turned from the waves. Jack grabbed his clothes and they began walking up the bluffs. Sam felt incredibly aware of Jack's big body sheltering hers from the light breeze. She'd enjoyed how he looked stripped down to shorts, all streaming wet flesh over hard sinew. She had to admit, tonight truly had been one of the wildest, most fun, most erotic experiences of her life, and all they'd done was kiss.

At her car, she turned to face him, leaning back against the Honda Civic she'd had for way too many years. "'Night."

He smiled that smile that started with his eyes and ended with his body, making hers hum. "'Night."

Since he just stood up there looking at her, she put out her hand.

A slow laugh escaped him, and he took her hand, using it to tug her against him.

He dropped his clothes on the hood of the car, pulled her close and gave her a scorching, scalding, blow-her-away kiss that left her shaky and relieved to have the car behind her when it ended.

She leaned on it with all her weight and felt the urge to revise her no-sleeping-with-a-date-on-the-first-night rule, because damn, she wanted more. She wanted him.

"What's on your mind?" He stroked a finger over her jaw.

She laughed, then shook her head.

"Nothing? Nothing's on your mind?"

"Oh, there's something there, it's just not up for public view."

His smile was slow and cocky as he shook out his pants, then put them on. His shirt was next. He held his shoes. "Really."

"Really." But because he looked so delicious— his body still damp and practically steaming— standing there in his bare feet, she hooked her finger in his unbuttoned shirt and tugged him back.

"More?" he whispered.

"Just a little." And she brought his mouth back to hers.

His shoes hit the gravel and both arms encircled her, gliding up her back, into her hair, which was still dripping.

This kiss was even deeper, wetter, hotter....

And harder to let go. But eventually it had to end and she pulled back, staring up into his face, a little stunned at how difficult it was to do so.

Okay, maybe just a little more—

But before she could say a word, he reached over, opened her door—clucking over the fact she hadn't locked it—and helped her inside.

Never in her life had she been so aware of a man's touch as when his hand settled low on her spine. It made her want to turn and face him, and see what other reactions he could cause within her.

But she didn't, and he waited until she started the engine and pulled on her seat belt before stepping back.

And then, with nothing else to do, she drove away. She drove into the night, going north along the coast highway for a good half hour. She might have even ended up in Santa Barbara if she hadn't eventually stopped for gas, grabbed another soda and then gotten on the road, heading south again.

She did a lot of thinking, too much for a woman

who wasn't fond of introspection. That led to painful thoughts, regretful thoughts...sad thoughts. She always avoided those.

The ocean was a black heaving mass on her right. The Malibu Hills a dark outline on her left. Nothing to keep her mind from wandering.

It had been an incredible evening. She wanted more evenings like that, with Jack.

There.

She'd put it into words. For the first time in too long, she'd met a guy who had made her look beyond just this one date.

Scary stuff.

6

THE NEXT MORNING, Sam sat on her surfboard in the same water she'd swum with Jack only a few hours before. Lorissa perched on her own board alongside, and as they watched their friends and fellow surfers ride some waves, they talked.

Or rather Lorissa talked, hounding Sam for the scoop on the night before.

But oddly enough, Sam didn't feel like giving any details, even though the thought of Jack still put a grin on her face.

"Come on, tell me something." Lorissa's body rose and fell gently as a swell rode beneath them.

"I told you, I had fun."

"I need more than that."

"I'll tell you this wave is mine." Sam started paddling to catch it, then heaved herself up to her feet.

When she got back to Lorissa, she wasn't alone. Skurfer, an old high school buddy who owned the surf shop they all went to, smiled. "Did you score last night?" he wanted to know.

"We're what, eight years out of school? Can't we come up with a better term than *score*?"

"Sure." This from Nash, another of their long-time friends, and Sam's old middle-school crush. He offered them an alternative word, a four-letter universal term, and everyone laughed.

Except Lorissa. Still straddling her board, she put her hands on her hips. "Sam did not *score* with a blind date. She's too careful for that." She looked at Sam. "Right?"

"Right." Sam eyed the incoming set of waves with newfound determination, because maybe riding them, she could get some peace. "And if whoever's next in line doesn't hurry up and take more interest in these breakers than my sex life, then they're going to lose."

The guys went together, while Lorissa and Sam watched.

"You didn't sleep with him," Lorissa said in a low tone.

"Is that a guess?"

Lorissa eyed her for a long time. "No, it's the truth. You like sex as much as anyone I know, but oddly enough for someone who doesn't want to be in a relationship, you need more than one date to get intimate. You didn't sleep with him, I'd bet my next paycheck on it."

No, she hadn't. But God, she'd wanted to. "You know that for sure, huh?"

"Well, it's not like you've changed your policy over the years. Like I said, rule number one, you don't sleep with a guy until you know him. Rule number two, you scratch your itch and dump him."

"Hey. I don't—"

"Yes, you do." Lorissa's smile was sad. "We both know by the time you like a guy enough to sleep with him, it's the kiss of death for that relationship because you don't like being part of a couple. Relationships scare you."

"Would you stop with the *R* word?"

"What's the matter, am I making you jittery?"

Sam sighed. "I'm taking this one." She started paddling toward the next wave.

"You're taking it because you know I'm right," Lorissa called after her.

"I'm going because this is a good one—"

"Was he a jerk?"

Startled, Sam glanced back and saw real worry in Lorissa's eyes.

"Because if he was," she called out. "I'll kill him. And I'll kill Cole, too, who vouched for him. I'll kill them both, slowly."

Sam looked up into the perfect wave cresting, and…let it go.

With a sigh, she paddled back to where Lorissa sat in her patriotic red, white and blue bandeau top and ancient, shredded blue surfer shorts, straddling the board that Sam had bought her for Christmas three years ago. Concern, fear and regret were stamped all over her.

Sam's heart tightened. Last night while driving along the coast, she'd had that burst of feeling isolated, and yet she wasn't alone at all.

So what made it so hard to reach out, to accept love? She had no idea, but she reached out now, because the truth was, the only reason she'd been able to go on after losing her parents had been because of the woman looking at her right this minute. Lorissa had loved and bullied and loved her some more, more than anyone else all these years. "He wasn't a jerk. Not even close. In fact, he was…" Heavenly. Delicious. Magnificent. "A perfect gentleman," she said finally.

Even when he'd stripped off his clothes and dove into the ocean, with that long, lean, hard heat rubbing up against her—

"Okay." Lorissa cocked her head, searching Sam's expression carefully. "So why all the secrecy— Oh. Oh, damn," she breathed softly. "You like him. You really like him." Lorissa's face split into a wide grin. "Tell me the truth."

Sam should have taken that wave. "I had a

good time," she admitted, and when Lorissa just waited, she sighed. "Fine. Make that a *great* time."

"So you're going to see him again? Has he called? Have you called? Stop holding back on me, damn it!"

"It's only been a few hours. And *you're* the one who should spill, you neglected to tell me he was an ex-NBA star."

"Actually, I didn't know." Lorissa looked thoughtful. "I guess I should have matched his name with the stories." She shrugged. "I've never been much for watching basketball."

Yeah, neither had Sam.

"So…what's next? Another date? Or did you give him the famous Sam Blow-Off?"

"Well…next weekend we're doing this…thing."

"Omigod, you're going on date number two!" Lorissa looked as though she'd just won the lottery.

"I'm just helping him and his sister at some charity carnival. That's all. Not really date number two."

"Uh-huh."

"It's not." Giving up convincing Lorissa when she couldn't even convince herself, Sam took the next wave.

ON MONDAY, Sam skipped her morning surf to make her monthly trek out to San Juan Capistrano.

As she had on the first Monday of every month

without fail for five years, she got out of her car at the secluded little house on the beach, walked up the steps and knocked.

And pulled a check from her purse written from her checking account for just enough money to make her wince—especially after dropping $800 on Jack Knight at the auction.

The door opened and there stood Red—a sixty-five-year-old, lanky lean, skin-tanned-to-leather, long-haired beach bum. The beach bum who'd given her a job when she'd been fourteen with too much free time on her hands.

The same beach bum who was her mother's older brother, a man who'd never wanted children and yet had taken her in when her parents died, giving her what he could when life had taken so much away.

And as always, just the sight of Red caught her by the chest and squeezed.

In return, his light blue eyes twinkled and warmed. But he was duty-bound by habit to give her his monthly scowl as he leaned against the doorjamb, arms crossed. "Is it that time already?"

"You know it is."

"Yeah. So what do you want?"

Grabbing his hand, she slapped the check into his palm. "What do you think?"

He peered down at the piece of paper, and as

it did every month, his scowl deepened. "Is it any good?"

"Deposit it and see."

"Maybe I don't want to go to the trouble."

Nothing ever changed about this dialogue. As always, he tried to hand the check back to her.

She put her hands behind her back. "What's the matter, my money not good enough for you?"

"I keep telling you I don't want your money."

"I bought your place, I'm paying for your place. You hold the mortgage. How many times do we have to go through this? Just deposit the damn check and reduce my damn debt, and soon enough I'll stop showing up on your doorstep."

"Fine." He jammed the check into the pocket of his faded Hawaiian surf shorts, which hung low on his skinny hips. "I suppose you've been staying out of trouble."

"I suppose." She peered in past him to look at the small place he'd been slowly renovating now that he'd retired. "You hire a maid for this sty yet?"

"Yep, with your money, thanks. Sure you don't want to take the check back?" He looked at her with some amusement. "You could buy yourself some cooking lessons. Learn to make brownies."

"Ha, ha." Everyone knew about her determination to make decent brownies.

And really, the urge made perfect sense. Any

psychiatrist would have had a field day with it—
her mother had always made brownies, and
they'd always been perfect and scrumptious.

Sam knew deep down she wrecked her own
batches on purpose. She must have a thing against
being truly happy, or wanting real love, or being
afraid…something stupid like that.

She didn't care. She still tried to make brownies the way her mom had.

"Well, then, maybe buy yourself some new
clothes," Red suggested, eyeing her denim cut-
offs, tank top and flip-flops. "Or even get a hair
cut. Find yourself a man."

"Shows what you know. I don't need to get new
clothes or trim my hair to get a man."

"Uh-huh. I see you've got yourself a real big
rock on that marrying finger."

She glanced down at her ringless hands and
rolled her eyes. "I'm not interested in getting mar-
ried. Why would I be?"

"Maybe because I'd like to see you happy and
taken care of."

Everything within her softened. Still she had
her tough facade to keep up. "I can make *myself*
happy, thank you very much, and I certainly can
take care of myself."

"Really? You've got it all covered, huh?"

She lifted her chin. "You bet."

"And kids? You going to give yourself kids?"

"Look, I didn't come all the way down here to get a lecture."

"Then why are you still standing here?"

Because he was the closest thing to a father she had, and sometimes she just liked to look at him. "Traffic's a bitch. I figured you'd want to feed me the leftovers you'd just be throwing away anyway."

"I suppose." He stood back, gestured her in with a jerk of his head.

The moment she reached the top step, he put his hand on her shoulder, then pulled her in for a big hug. She dropped her tough stance and held on tightly.

"Leftovers that I'd be throwing away?" he murmured, his body shaking as he let out a belly laugh. "Have I ever fed you leftovers?"

"No, because thankfully you're such an awesome cook there are rarely leftovers for more than an hour." She grinned.

"Then I suppose it's lucky for you I just put together lunch."

"Oh, really?" She batted her eyes, making him laugh again, because they both knew he'd planned on her coming and that, as always, he'd made them a meal.

"Come on," he said, and drew her inside, toward the kitchen that smelled delicious. "And tell me what's new."

She did exactly that, leaving out only the news of her date with Jack Scandal Knight, probably for the same reason she hadn't spilled all to Lorissa—she had no idea what exactly to say.

FOR A YEAR NOW, Jack had been concentrating on keeping a low profile, on just amusing himself. He'd been pretty damn successful at it, too. He hung out with friends, rode his bike for miles every morning. Lately, he'd been spending more time with the kids Heather helped, and at the old rec center. And most recently, he'd been organizing and coaching basketball teams.

He'd been content with that, or as content as he could be. But then had come his blind date with Sam. It didn't make any sense that he couldn't stop thinking about her. She'd run with him from the reporters, she'd made the charity event fun—not an easy feat—and then later… Her kisses had made him so hot, and those little sounds she'd made in the back of her throat when he touched her, even hotter.

Not to mention bodysurfing half-naked by moonlight on a first date. That had been a welcome first. In comparison, his slow, unplanned life seemed just a tad boring. Maybe he was ready for the next phase of retirement, whatever that might be.

He hoped it included Sam.

He had looked up the number for Wild Cherries, but when he'd called, no one answered. Later, he had driven by the place, but it had been closed.

Seemed even beach girls took days off. Which was too bad because their next date seemed a long way off.

What he really needed was a distraction. And thankfully Monday night was poker night with his buddies. This was their chance to get together and blow off steam—a time to vent and forget that they were all famous celebrities, athletes, politicians… Every week, they took as much joy in razzing each other for whatever headlines they'd shown up in that week as they did in actually playing cards.

This week, Jack was the host. Cole showed up first. As always, he came dressed to be seen, wearing expensive clothes with a casual air that always boggled Jack's mind. Jack dressed up only when he had to. They'd become friends in college while sharing a dorm room, and though they'd led vastly different lives, Jack in basketball, and Cole in marketing, they'd remained tight. Mostly because Cole never deferred to Jack's celebrity status, and never talked B.S. Two traits not easily found in Jack's world.

Cole slapped a stack of magazines against Jack's chest and headed straight for the vodka behind the bar. "You're going to suffer tonight, buddy."

Jack looked down at the magazines in his hands. He'd made a few covers. Splashed across *People*, *US Weekly* and a handful of others, were shots of Jack piggybacking Sam in her little black dress across the rolling grass hills at the country club.

Another set showed them at the buffet table, oblivious to the upscale crowd around them, sharing some food, their heads close enough to kiss. On his face was a look he hardly recognized.

Pleasure.

He didn't quite know how to describe his expression in the next photo, where he was tugging Sam out of the club, other than that it was one of sheer determination, hunger and pure, unadulterated lust. "Oh boy."

"Yeah." Cole swallowed his first shot, set the glass on the bar and smiled. "She's something. You can thank me any time. You going to do her?"

"Shut up, Cole."

Cole stopped in the act of pouring another shot. He looked Jack over for a long moment. "So the pictures *are* telling the truth."

"What truth?"

"You're into her."

"I don't know what I am."

"No?" Cole toasted him with his glass. "Well,

you'd better figure it out before the other guys get here, or they'll tear you apart."

They tore him apart anyway until he lost all dignity. And in a sign of how far he'd lost his edge, he also nearly lost his shirt, too.

ON TUESDAY, Jack refereed three boys' basketball games and then, needing a different kind of connection, tried calling Sam again—yet another sign of how far gone he was. While he sat in his car listening to the phone ringing, he tried to create a mental list of the things that had bothered him about her, his usual MO for *not* having date number two.

But his list turned up short. In fact, it was non-existent.

"Hello," she answered breathlessly.

"Sam, it's Jack."

Silence.

"Jack Knight," he said, and felt very stupid.

"I remember who you are, Jack. The first man I've ever bodysurfed with at midnight."

An idiotic grin split his face. The first? He liked that, he liked that far too much. "So how are you?" he asked, discovering that the usual easy conversation starter, the one that had always meant nothing, suddenly mattered. He really did want to know how she was.

"I'm up to my elbows in brownie mix if you want the truth, and this time, I have a good feeling about it."

"Why? Do you usually have a problem with brownies?"

She sighed. "I make the best sandwiches under the sun. Cookies, too. But I'm an utter failure at brownies. Today, I break the curse."

"Want a personal taster?"

"You mean…"

"For brownies, I'd drive to China. I'll come over and sample them for you."

"No! I mean, I'm not sure that's a good idea. I've never managed a good batch yet."

"If they're awful, I promise I won't even mention it."

"Look, I— No. No, thank you. I'm sorry—"

His grin faded. He'd misread everything. "No, it's okay. I understand—"

"It's just that the other night was so…" She let out a breath.

"Yeah." From stupid to mortified.

"So I guess I'm just hoping that by Saturday, I'll see you and realize I've just exaggerated how much fun you were."

Suddenly, he didn't feel anything but good, damn good. "Best of luck with the brownies, Sam."

"The brownies—" Something clanged in his ear, and he realized she'd dropped the phone. He waited, and when she came back, she was irritated. "Got to have that oven checked. The damn thermostat is out and it's over-cooking everything."

"Blaming the oven?"

"What? You want to hear that you distracted me and *I* overcooked them? You've been distracting me for days. Go away, Jack. And stay out of my head until Saturday. *Please.*"

"I will if you will."

"You're having the same problem?"

She sounded far more wary than amused, and his own pleasure faded, replaced by other emotions he didn't want to face. "See you Saturday," he said softly, and hung up.

He lasted two days, during which he kept himself busy organizing and registering basketball players for a kids' league at the rec center before he called Wild Cherries again. He'd have called her at home, but didn't have that number. He liked that she hadn't given it to him—it meant she'd been utterly honest about being commitment phobic, which was always a damned attractive trait in a woman.

And yet his heart had started a heavy, excited beat at the thought of hearing her voice again.

"Wild Cherries," she answered the phone, sounding breathless. "Can I help you?"

"Sam."

"Hey." There was a smile in her voice, and suddenly there was one on his face as well.

"Just wanted to hear you."

"You're hearing me. What's up?"

"You surf today?"

"Yeah." She covered the mouthpiece to speak to someone, but he could still hear her. "Knock it off, Nash, I am not going to tell him that."

"Tell me what?"

"I made the mistake of serving a few friends some lunch and now they're being obnoxious."

"What did they want you to tell me?"

She hesitated, then laughed. "That they'll, and I quote, kick your butt if you hurt me. They don't realize they're threatening Jack Scandal Knight."

"Holy crap," said an awed voice.

Sam laughed. "As for surfing, it was rough today, and I got my butt kicked out there. Lorissa had a great time laughing at me when I face-planted right in front of her."

"You okay?"

"Not a scratch. How about you? What are you up to?"

Thinking of you. "Lost at poker the other night. Badly."

"Ouch. You should play me sometime, it will make you feel better about yourself." She laughed. "I'm horrible. Last time I played strip poker—"

He choked out a laugh. "I was *not* playing strip poker with the guys."

"Oh." She laughed, too. "Of course not. So how about that weather, huh?"

"Oh, no, we're not changing the subject, yet. About this strip poker thing…"

"It was a long time ago," she said primly now, though he could still hear the smile in her voice.

"How about we rectify that?"

"Are you suggesting—"

"Definitely I'm suggesting. We play. I'll give you pointers."

"Uh-huh."

"Hey, I have your best interests in mind."

Her soft chuckle was outrageously sexy. "Maybe some other time," she said. "Did you see the magazines?"

He sighed. "Yeah. Sorry."

"Don't be. A customer actually asked me for an autograph today. Famous for a day, at least."

"You're being an incredibly good sport."

"That's life, right?"

"It is, isn't it. You know what? You're just what I needed today."

"Yeah?" She sounded pleased.

"Yeah."

"So…I'll see you on Saturday?"

"Unless I could talk you into that poker game. Tonight."

"Not tonight. Not…yet."

But she didn't say not ever. She asked him about Heather then, and he asked her about her latest sandwich creation, and before he knew it an hour had gone by, and she had to go because apparently Lorissa was getting irritated about handling the café while Sam chatted on the phone with him.

That night, he dreamed about holding her hot and wet in his arms, just as when they'd body-surfed, talking and laughing, kissing. And despite not getting her into bed, that first date had rivaled any night he'd ever spent with a woman; in fact, it ranked up there as the hottest, most sensual night of his life.

SATURDAY CAME before Sam knew it. The morning was chilly and foggy, but that didn't stop her from surfing and swimming with Lorissa and the gang as usual. When they were done, Lorissa opened the café and Sam went upstairs to get ready for the carnival.

"Stop it," she told her overly excited reflection in the bathroom mirror. "He's just a guy."

Yeah, just a guy. A very gorgeous guy who

made her laugh and could kiss her every last brain cell away.

Not today, she told herself. Today was just for the kids. Today, he would irritate her in some way, surely he would. And then she'd be free from thinking of him, of dreaming of him.

She heard gravel crunch as a car pulled into the parking lot, and ran to the window, pressing her nose to the glass to catch sight of Jack's Escalade. Her stomach tightened.

So much for irritating her. But the day was young yet, and she'd never gone through an entire second date without wanting to ditch the guy. So really it was only a matter of time.

7

SAM RAN DOWN the stairs of her apartment and through Wild Cherries, planting herself at the counter as casually as she could, just as Jack walked through the gate and stepped onto the patio.

Calm, she reminded herself. Remain calm. At least it was a cool morning. Usually the thermometer hanging above her head had neared ninety by now, if not more, but today it was only seventy.

And yet, just seeing Jack sent her inner temperature off the chart.

Because of the cooler weather, the café had stolen the beach crowd and was filled with people looking for hot tea and coffee instead of the usual juices and iced tea. Sam knew Lorissa and the two high school kids she'd hired this season could handle the café in her absence.

In fact, Lorissa stood only a few feet away, on the other side of the counter, rag in hand as she wiped it down. She lifted her brow, signaling she'd seen not only Jack's arrival, but Sam's run through the place.

Skurfer was sitting a few tables away with some of his buddies, and by his smirk, he'd seen, too. She grimaced back, but her heart did a backflip as Jack walked through the filled tables directly toward her. He wore a white polo shirt, San Diego Eels sweat pants that buttoned down the outside of his legs, mirrored sunglasses and an unreadable expression.

She sat there on a bar stool, her pulse frantically beating in her ears. Lorissa set two mugs of hot chocolate in front of her. "Careful," she whispered. "You're drooling."

"Yeah, yeah." Sam watched Jack come close and took a deep breath. "Hey," she said, as casually as she could.

"Hey, yourself." A slow smile lit his face, and he shoved the sunglasses to the top of his head. His eyes were smiling, too, and she decided that was a good look on him.

Very good.

He draped his tall frame on the stool next to hers, accepting the drink when she slid it over to him. "Thanks." He took a sip. "It's not as warm today as I'd hoped."

Maybe not, but it was sure hot in here, she thought, watching his Adam's apple slide up and down as he drank.

He reached over, taking her hand, holding it away from her as he looked her over.

She wore a sundress today, the same color as the sea. She knew the thin, wispy material of the dress played peekaboo with the bathing suit she wore beneath it and also knew that she looked quite passable.

The heat in his eyes told her she may have pulled off more than quite passable.

"Another dress over a bathing suit," he said after drinking some more.

"I took the words *dunking booth* to heart."

"Yeah." He sighed. "I'm hoping she's just messing with me." He stood and, still holding her hand, pulled her to her feet as well.

"I guess we're going to find out."

"Yeah."

Because his smile had faded, hers did as well. "What's the matter, Jack?"

He shook his head, then brought his free hand up to her face to sink into the hair she'd left free and flowing over her shoulders.

Out of the corner of her eye, she knew Lorissa was watching their every move.

"I thought about you all damn week," Jack murmured.

That took her breath. So did the light kiss he dropped on her lips. "Let's go?"

"Yes," she said. Incredibly aware of the interested gazes of the people around them, she couldn't admit that she'd been thinking about him, too.

Every single living second.

"Have fun." Lorissa took their cups away. "Be careful."

They walked to the parking lot. Jack opened the passenger door for her, but instead of sliding in, she looked up into his eyes. "I thought of you, too." She shut the door on his surprised expression.

When he came around to the driver's seat, he didn't say a word, thank God. He didn't have to, his smile said it all.

Have fun, Lorissa had said. *Be careful.*

Right. Only there was no way she could she do both at the same time, not with this man.

THE CARNIVAL WAS abuzz with preopening activity. Jack stared at their booth. "She really meant it."

Sam laughed. There were wild rides and row upon row of games, where you could lose as much money as you wanted, and more. There were arts and crafts booths as well, and a wide variety of food stands selling high-fat fast food. On the walk to their booth Jack had been stopped a few times for autographs, and though he did it happily enough, he deflected any personal questions, private as always.

Music filled the salty air, blaring out of speakers set up at the end of every row. Sam found herself grinning with anticipation and excitement as she eyed the dunking booth in front of them. A large tank of water sat beneath a bench that looked rather like a diving board, and above it, a bull's-eye for people to throw softballs at. When one hit the mark, the seat—with one of them on it— would drop. "Look on the bright side," she said. "That's a long throw and a rather small target. No kid is actually going to be able to hit that. We'll be dry all day."

"Yeah? Why don't you go first and make sure. In fact, I'll throw first, just to check it out."

"Oh, no," she said, laughing, backing up a little at the wicked look in his eyes. "You should go first."

"And why is that?"

"Um…" To see if he looked as good wet in the daylight as he had by moonlight? "To make sure it's safe," she came up with brilliantly.

He laughed knowingly, and when his cell phone rang, he flipped it open. "What now, Heather? Uh-huh…listen, didn't we just see you three minutes ago sitting on your throne at the ticket booth collecting money?" His eyes shot to Sam's. "You're opening for business and you need my butt on the hot spot? Gee, thanks. Yeah, yeah, love you, too, but I wouldn't sleep with both eyes shut tonight if I were you." He snapped the phone shut, slid it into his pants pocket and looked at the dunking booth with what could only be dread.

Sam had to laugh. "I know you're not afraid of water."

He cut his gaze back to her as he kicked off his shoes and then tugged off his sweats. Beneath he wore knee-length dark blue swim trunks. "I'm not afraid of anything," he said, and pulled off his shirt.

She worked on not swallowing her tongue. As she'd seen the week before, the man hadn't lost any of his muscle tone in the year since he'd stopped playing. She'd made it her business to look up and learn about his career this past week. He'd been a true athlete, one of the best, until multiple knee injuries and the subsequent surgeries had taken him off the top of his game. He claimed not to be afraid of anything, but she knew better—because he'd told her himself. "Except commitment," she reminded him. "You're afraid of commitment."

His shirt hit her in the face. When she pulled it away, after first gulping in a big breath to catch his delicious scent, he lifted a brow.

"Isn't that a bit like the pot calling the kettle black?"

She lifted her chin.

"Fine," he said. "Neither of us like to admit being afraid of anything. We're big, bad toughies with an impenetrable surface." He walked toward the ladder that would take him to the hot seat. "But I'll bet your sweet ass that my impenetrable surface is going to freeze right off if anyone manages a hit."

"Don't worry," she crooned, struggling to hold back a laugh at the look on his face as he sat there, tanned and sleek and shirtless, his long legs dangling down nearly to the level of water, looking like he'd rather have an enema. Poor baby. "I'll bet that water isn't that cold."

"I'll be sure to let you know." He eyed the crowd now running in from the main gates. Before another minute passed, there was a long line of kids waiting to dunk Jack Scandal Knight.

Secretly, Sam hoped someone got him. She wanted to see that finely honed-to-perfection body all wet and gleaming. She wanted that a lot.

The first kid was a young girl, maybe seven years old. Sam took her tickets, and in return gave her two softballs. "Dunk him," Sam said. "He can't wait to hit the water."

The girl's first throw fell short of the tank. She thrust out her lower lip and looked up at Sam with determination in her eyes. "I wanna dunk him."

Sam pulled the girl over the line, and a good five feet closer to Jack. "Try again."

"Hey," Jack protested.

Sam smiled sweetly at him. "Hey, back."

The girl missed again.

Sam thought she heard Jack's relieved sigh flutter over the air.

The next kid was a young teen and looked to have a good arm on him. Sam handed him two balls. "Dunk him."

"I will," he promised, and his first ball hit the very edge of the target, but bounced away without releasing the seat.

"Come on, you can do it," she said, avoiding looking at Jack while the kid wound up for ball number two.

"Sam?"

This from Jack.

The kid paused in his throw.

Sam looked at Jack.

"For every kid you encourage to dunk me," he said silkily, "I'm going to buy a ball when you're up here, and believe me, I'm not going to miss, not once."

Everyone in line laughed.

Sam's stomach dropped to her toes. "That might be expensive. And besides, I wouldn't want you to throw like that. You might hurt your shoulder. In fact, I'll make a warning sign because, now that I think about it, retirees shouldn't play at this booth. Too dangerous to their health."

More laughter.

Jack's face broke slowly into an extremely evil smile. "Oh, don't you worry about my health, sweetheart. I might be retired, but I'm still in full working order."

Sam's hormones jumped.

The young teen threw his second ball.

And down Jack went. The splash he made had the kids hooting and hollering, and when he surfaced, he tossed back his wet hair and looked right at her. He continued to do so as he effortlessly pulled himself back up and reset the seat.

Dripping wet.

Glistening.

Looking like the pagan god of sin, with water streaming down his body and those glittering eyes on hers, he smiled at her with pure wickedness.

She swallowed hard. "Next," she squeaked.

A young woman stood there, clearly as in awe of Jack as Sam was. She licked her lips and made sure she was as close to the line as she could get. "I'm standing here until I dunk him," she told Sam. "I don't care how much money it takes."

It took five bucks.

And this time when Jack climbed back up, he looked at Sam and mouthed, "Two."

She blinked.

"That's two people you've gotten to dunk

me," he clarified. "Don't think I'm not keeping track."

"It's my job," she said weakly, but when she handed balls to the next person in line—another young woman—Sam didn't offer one word of encouragement.

When she missed, Sam breathed a sigh of relief.

But then came the most adorable little girl ever. She couldn't be more than four, with long dark hair and the darkest eyes Sam had ever seen. She was clutching the hand of a woman wearing the official tag of Heather's charity.

"This is one of our kids," the woman said. "Thelma is in a group home near the rec center, and some of the money we earn here today will go toward new play equipment in her yard."

Sam looked down into Thelma's dark eyes and felt her heart crack. "Well, then, sweetie, this game is on me."

"I get a ball?"

"You get as many balls as it takes to dunk Jack Knight," Sam rashly promised, and pulled a twenty out of her pocket to add to the day's earnings. Then she picked Thelma up and tucked her on her hip. With her other hand she grabbed a basket of balls and stepped over the line. "Dunk him."

Thelma giggled, and threw her first ball, which went about three feet.

Sam stepped even closer to the tank, and the target. She met Jack's eyes.

He lifted a brow. "Three, Sam?"

She thrust her chin in the air. "Again, Thelma."

Thelma missed.

Sam moved even closer.

The crowd was cheering loudly now. Jack looked both intrigued by Sam's interference, and also quite resigned.

The third throw was beautiful. Thelma hit the target and Jack took another bath.

When he surfaced this time, he didn't climb back onto his seat. He got out of the tank. He didn't grab a towel; he came directly toward Sam, who was just about to put Thelma down, but suddenly felt holding the thin, warm body close was a good idea. "Thelma, what do you say we go—"

"Hi, there." Jack bent a little and smiled into Thelma's eyes. "Do you know who I am?"

"You fly through the air and you make baskets."

Jack laughed, and so did the people around them. "I did," he agreed. "And now I'm going to make this pretty lady holding you fly. Right into the water, like I just did. Do you want to see that?"

Thelma clapped her hands.

Sam's heart started beating as fast as a hummingbird's wings. Faster. "Well, I don't really think Thelma wants to get down right now—"

Thelma opened her arms to Jack.

Wet and all, he took the little girl from Sam and smiled sweetly down into her face. "That's a girl. Want to help me?"

Thelma nodded.

And everyone looked expectantly at Sam.

"I don't think I ever agreed to actually get into the tank," she said, glancing over at the water, which suddenly looked very, very cold. "I'm pretty sure I just said I'd help."

"Yes, and this is going to be a great help," Jack told her. "Seeing you in a bathing suit, and wet, will help me tremendously." He waggled a brow challengingly. "Unless you want to chicken out, of course." He smiled down at Thelma, happy in his arms. "I'm sure the kids will understand if you don't want to—"

"Oh, fine." Stepping back, she untied the strap of her halter sundress from around her neck, unzipped it and let it fall. She kicked it up to Jack, who caught it and grinned at her, taking in her white bikini.

Reaching up, she gathered her hair, tying it with the band she'd had around her wrist. Ready, she paused to take one last look at Jack and then went still.

His eyes, hot and hungry, were right on hers.

And her heart, racing only a second before, skipped a beat. And then another.

"Don't worry," he said lightly. "The water's only a little cold."

"Thanks." Moving to the tank, she climbed the ladder while everyone cheered her on.

And then she was sitting on the little seat—wet from Jack's body—waiting to be dunked.

She watched Jack run his free hand over Thelma's hair before he grabbed a ball. He said something to the crowd over his shoulder, and everyone in line cracked up.

She rolled her eyes. She'd gotten him dunked, and now he was going to follow through on his threat and do the same to her. It was a male thing, an ego thing, a *stupid* male ego thing, so really, she had no idea why her stomach did a funny little quiver, why her thighs tightened, why her whole body was heating up.

Unbelievable, but all this silly little playing back and forth was turning her on.

She needed a therapist, she decided as Jack tossed the ball up and down in his hand, smiling at her.

He wound up.

And with perfect aim, dunked her on his first try.

She went down with a startled squeal that had Jack grinning broadly. Beneath the water she became a blur, then her long legs gave a strong kick and she surfaced. Shaking the water from her face, she didn't look at him as she climbed out of the tank.

But he looked at her.

And looked.

Those long, toned limbs, all that dripping wet flesh…

Oh yeah, today was looking up.

Thelma laughed and clapped her hands. "More."

Jack laughed. "You've got it sweetheart."

AT THE END of the day, Sam's body was humming with a pleasant sort of exhaustion. Hair still damp, she slid into the passenger seat of Jack's SUV and put her head back.

"Tired?" Jack poured himself into his seat, not uttering a word or complaint about his right knee, which she'd caught him favoring a few times. "Because I'm beat to hell. Who'd of thought dunking you would have done me in."

"I warned you," she said. "The sport is dangerous for retirees."

He slanted her a daring look. "Are you asking me to somehow show you I am in no way ready for the old folks' home? Because that's what it sounds like, and believe me, this body is still in prime condition, and I'm willing to prove it."

She laughed. "Has a line like that ever actually worked for you?"

He rubbed his jaw, looking only a little sheepish. "Yeah."

Sam gave a slow shake of her head. "That's a sorry statement of my entire gender." But inside, her whole body continued to hum with excitement.

Jack started the car and they drove out of the lot. "I think Heather pulled in a ton of money today."

"Entertaining kids is a lot harder than I thought."

"You were a damn good sport about it." He glanced at her. "Thanks for—"

She laughed, shook her head. "Oh, no you don't."

"Oh, no I don't what?"

"You are not going to thank me."

"Uh…okay. Why not?"

She lifted a shoulder. "Because you were a good sport, too, and I'm not going to thank you. Everyone should give back to their community like that, and I'm ashamed to say I don't, not really. But I like the way I feel right now, so I'm going to try to change that."

He glanced at her but didn't say a word, not until he pulled into Wild Cherries. Turning off the engine, unhooking first his seat belt and then hers, he faced her. He slid his hands to hers when she might have gotten out of the car. "You're an amazing woman, Samantha O'Ryan. Anyone ever tell you that?"

She knew her smile was far too dreamy for her own comfort. "Stop it. You don't know me well enough to say that. You don't know the truth."

"And what's the truth?"

"I'm bossy, outspoken and don't follow rules very well." She squirmed a little. "Among other things."

"Yeah. So?" Lifting a hand, he tucked a wayward strand of hair behind her ear, then trailed his finger down her throat until her breath caught.

"That doesn't scare you?" she whispered.

"That you're bossy, outspoken and don't follow rules?" He looked into her eyes and laughed. "Maybe if you were my financial adviser, but no…" He traced her throat again, down to the very base of her neck where she knew her pulse had just leaped. "You don't scare me." He dipped his head and kissed the spot his finger had just touched.

The feel of his lips on her had her head falling back a little, her eyes closing. She told herself that the reason she didn't scare him because this…this *thing* between them wasn't going anywhere. Nowhere except quite possibly—hopefully—to the bedroom, and they both understood that.

She repeated it to herself to make sure she got it. This wasn't going anywhere. Neither of them wanted any such connection. No matter how many times she said it, however, it didn't seem to ring true, which led her to a bigger dilemma. Was this more than just girl meets boy, girl enjoys boy for summer, then girl moves on?

No. This was temporary only. Fun. Uninhibited. And at the moment, with his mouth cruising its way over her collarbone, hair brushing the underside of her chin, his hands on her hips, that worked for her. That worked really well.

Even though she suspected she'd need another pep talk soon enough. "Jack?"

He'd made his way to her shoulder, bared by her sundress, and he gave her a playful nip that he promptly soothed with a kiss. "Hmm?"

"Want to come in?"

He went still, then lifted his head and met her gaze. "For…another hot chocolate?"

"Not exactly." She winced. "I don't just work here. I, uh…live above the café."

"You do?"

"Yeah. I don't usually like guys to know because…"

"Because then maybe they'd show up when you didn't want them to," he guessed.

"Yeah. I'm sorry I didn't tell you."

"I understand, believe me, I do."

She imagined he did, for close to the same reasons. "I have some herbal lotion upstairs, made by a friend who really knows what she's doing. I could put some on your sore knee, see if it helps."

He blinked once, slow as an owl.

"I mean, unless you have something else—" Feeling silly, she turned away, reached for the door handle, but he stopped her and turned her back to face him.

"I'd love to come up."

8

THE EARLY EVENING ocean breeze had kicked in. It whistled over Sam and Jack, along with the sounds of the waves hitting the beach and the traffic on the highway.

Jack followed Sam up the back steps of the café to her apartment, watching as she pulled her keys from her tiny purse and unlocked the door. She stepped aside, holding it open for him, and in the swirling jade depths of her eyes he saw good humor, intelligence and…hunger. For him.

Thank God, he thought, and would have dug right in if it hadn't been for what he also saw there.

Affection.

Not the love-your-body, or make-me-feel-good-tonight kind of affection, nothing as shallow or as easy as that, but something far more, far deeper. He took a shuddering breath, wondering how to react.

A part of him wanted to run like hell.

Another part wanted to stand still and do as he'd never done before—absorb it, go with it.

Nurture it.

Clearly he was losing his mind. No woman had ever really gotten to know him for his sake, and no woman was likely to start. Not even Sam, who lived on the busy highway above a cramped lunch café and didn't seem to care about his celebrity or money—a woman who, until a week ago, wouldn't have known him from any other Jack.

But she knew who he was now, and if he'd learned anything over the years of being hounded by the public, by the press, by every single person around him, few people were unaffected by his celebrity.

Nope. As he'd told her during their midnight swim, he didn't want a relationship, no matter how tempting. Glorious as Sam was, and stimulating and beautiful and amazing, that hadn't changed.

"Stop thinking so hard, Jack," she said softly. "This isn't complicated. I just want to help soothe your pain."

Another confusion, as he hadn't told her his knee ached today. In fact, they hadn't really talked about that, or what he used to do for a living. She had just teased him about being retired.

He was used to dates who expected him to be the "star" the press had made him out to be. The simple truth was, women liked his celebrity, they wanted the perks that went along with it, and they expected him to provide them.

He'd known from the very beginning that Sam would be different. She still had no idea how damn attractive that had been to him. But now she'd casually mentioned his knee, which meant she had more than just a passing knowledge of him.

"You're not going to fit in here very well, it's really tiny." She took his hand and pulled him into the kitchen, which though as small as a closet, was warm and inviting. The floors were scarred hardwood but clean. Her table was made of wood, too, with two mismatched chairs that somehow worked in the place. Her cabinets had no fronts. Inside them, everything was neat as a pin.

"How long have you lived here?" he asked.

She lifted a shoulder. "Since I started working for Red full-time."

"Your uncle?"

"Yeah. And when he retired a few years back, buying this building was a natural fit for me. Of course, I'm mortgaged to my ears and I'll be paying out of said ears even after I am dead and buried…" She laughed. "And sometimes the home budget means eating whatever's left over from downstairs, but it's a small price to pay to belong somewhere."

He'd paid cash for his multimillion dollar home

in the hills and hadn't thought twice about it. Having a ridiculous amount of money, he rarely looked at the prices of things, and he never, ever, had to eat leftovers to keep to his budget. Hell, he had no budget.

Sam looked at the chairs, then at his large frame and, with a small smile, shook her head. She led him out of the kitchen and into the living room, which was also small, warm and homey. Two bare windows looked out to the ocean. There were more beat-up wood floors here, and a surprisingly large, forest-green sofa that was plumped up with pillows and looked so inviting he nearly sighed.

The entire apartment couldn't have been more than six hundred square feet, not much more than his own huge large entrance hall, and yet he'd never felt more at home than he did right now.

"Sit," she said. "I'll be right back."

His body twitched at that promise, but when she came back, she hadn't slipped out of her clothes, she wasn't holding a condom between her teeth and she wasn't looking at him with heat in her eyes—all three fantasies which had been whipping through his head since she'd disappeared.

In her hands was a pale green bottle. "The healing ointment," she said, and sat on the coffee table right in front of him, between his sprawled legs.

An unwittingly erotic position that made his fantasies even harder to let go of.

She looked into his eyes. "What's the matter?"

Other than being hard as a rock and you being oblivious to what you're doing to me, nothing. Nothing at all. "How did you know my knee is killing me? Or which one, for that matter."

"You're favoring your right one here and there." She opened the buttons down the sides of his sweats from mid-thigh to the hem. She uncapped the bottle and poured some of the stuff into her hands, rubbing them together, her gaze dropping to his right knee, and the six-inch-long scar running down the side of the kneecap.

"It smells awful," he said, wrinkling his nose.

"But it will feel heavenly." She put her hands on him, and he hissed in an involuntary breath.

"Cold? Sorry."

"No, it's…" Heavenly. Only he had no idea if that was because the stuff was soothing or because her hands were on him, rubbing slowly, so achingly slowly, that the rest of him wished it could cry out and feign hurt, too.

"How long since the surgery?" she asked quietly.

"The last one? Nearly eight months now. It's fine. It's healed."

"And yet you left basketball."

His gaze lifted from her fingers on his flesh up

to her eyes. "Fine and healed to walk are one thing. Fine and healed to play on a NBA court is another entirely."

"That must have destroyed you."

In all this time, no one had ever just put it out on the table like she just had, not even his family. Avoidance had been done in love and affection, but it had hurt regardless. "Yes," he said a little thickly, shocked to find his emotions so close to the surface. "It did for a while."

"So what do you do now? With your free time, I mean."

"Let the general public dunk me at carnivals."

"Surely you needn't have been forced out of basketball entirely. You could…I don't know. Coach. Announce. Ref—"

"I do. I run leagues and ref for the rec center. Not exactly demanding, I know, but the change of pace was good. Now I watch late night TV without worrying about curfew. I eat what I want, drink what I want. I exercise for fun instead of necessity, and I no longer have to answer to a committee on every little decision I make, including, but not limited to, what kind of shoes I wear and how many hours of sleep I get a night."

"That must be…freeing."

"Yeah. So is not having to be a role model when

I never asked to be one. So is walking onto a court and knowing there's no pressure, only fun."

"And you really don't miss it?"

Her heart was in her eyes. For him.

He stared down at her hands on his knee, and then put *his* hands on *her*, resting his palms on her thighs. Easy enough to do, since she sat between his sprawled legs. "I've something better to talk about. Massaging *you*, for instance."

She laughed. "I can't believe the lines you have. Do you expect me to fall for them? Really?"

"Are you saying you don't want me to return the favor?" Leaning in, he took a nibble out of her shoulder, gratified to hear her suck in her breath. "Because I've got great hands, Sam."

A helpless little moan escaped her when he started a trail of open-mouthed kisses back up to her throat. "Are you just trying to avoid talking?"

His hands gently squeezed her thighs and then moved to her waist. He lifted her from the table and set her on his lap.

Perfect. "Why would I do that?"

"I don't—" Another sexy little half whimper when he took the lobe of her ear lightly between his teeth. "I don't know."

"I have nothing against talking," he murmured, and made his way down her jaw, his hands encircling her, gliding up and down her slim spine.

"You talk all you want." Mouth to her ear now, he added, "While I kiss you from head to toe."

Laughing, she leaned away from him. "Your knee must feel all better."

"Actually…" He stretched it out. "Yes. Much."

She smiled sweetly. "Good." Rising, she grabbed the bottle and held it out to him. "You can take this with you. Rub it on a couple of times a day—"

Her words were cut off when he tugged her back down, pulled her against him and covered her mouth with his. A little overwhelmed, Sam went still for a second.

Apparently he took this for a challenge because he softened his hold immediately, as if instinctively knowing she could resist his aggressive hunger, but not slow and seductive desire…

He slid a hand into her hair at the nape of her neck, the other arm banding low on her hips, all while gently, tenderly, playing at her mouth with his knowing, talented one. He kissed one side, and then the other, and then slowly licked her lower lip until she let it tremble open.

And only then did he glide his tongue against hers in an age-old dance that had her hips mimicking the motion, and giving away what her mind had resisted but her body had no intention of withstanding.

"Your bathing suit is still damp." Over the material of her dress, his hand slipped down her back again, lower this time, over the curve of a buttock, which he palmed.

Her eyes drifted shut, and she let out a little shiver of anticipation.

"Cold?" he murmured, pulling her even closer, his hands warm on her body.

"No."

His gaze met hers, his fingers spread wide on her belly now, the very tips just brushing the underside of her breast, which tightened in its eagerness. "Sure?"

She nodded, silently admitting it wasn't a chill giving her goose bumps and hard nipples.

A soft smile curved his mouth, which he touched lightly to hers, just as the hand on her back softened its grip as well, soothing now as it stroked the length of her. "You really did invite me up here just to put that lotion on my knee, didn't you. Not to have wild, uninhibited sex—"

"That's right." She laughed, touched her forehead to his. "But I've thought about…wild, uninhibited sex. A lot. Does that count?"

"Oh, yeah." His sigh was long-suffering. "I guess it's another cold shower night for me."

That got a choked laugh out of her. "Another?"

"I spent a half hour in one after the midnight bodysurfing event."

"What, the ocean wasn't cold enough for you?"

"Not with you in it."

He saw a cocky smile break over her face, and he groaned. "Oh boy, now I've done it, I've given you even more power over me."

"I have a feeling you never let anyone have power over you," she said.

"Not often, I'll give you that. That lotion is good stuff. What other magic do you have?"

"That was it. My one trick."

Cocking his head, he studied her, a small smile playing on his lips. "I doubt that. You're an interesting woman, Sam. I like that. I like you."

"I'm not so interesting."

"You run a café that serves sandwiches like ham, seaweed, artichoke hearts and mozzarella cheese on whole wheat, and yet you can't make brownies to save your life. You're a natural around kids and yet the thought of settling down with a man in a relationship gives you hives—"

"You're not exactly one to talk—"

"But this is about you." He touched a finger to her cheek. "You're nervous dangling above a small tank of water and yet you'll surf in the ocean." Laughing, he shook his head. "A bundle of contradictions, but the sexiest bundle I've ever seen."

"You're not that different," she said, but her

words faded away when he ran a hand from her toes up her calf, to just beneath the material of her sundress. Breathing became a challenge.

"Really?" he whispered. His fingers played with the back of her knee in a way that made her want to let her legs fall open.

She kept them together by sheer will. "No. Not that different at all."

"How's that?" he asked softly, that little smile still dancing around his mouth. He knew exactly what he was doing to her. "Because I don't cook. And as for kids, I'm not a natural."

That made her laugh. "Yes, you are. Kids love you. They think you're a role model."

"I'm no one's role model."

"And yet children love you anyway." His fingers slipped up a few inches higher on the back of her leg, and her words stuttered to a halt. "Uh..." Where had she been? Oh, yes..."I know you had a hard time in the press, being labeled difficult—" Those fingers spread wide on the back of her thigh now. "A—and a prima donna." Now his fingers tightened imperceptibly before purposefully relaxing. Her gaze shot to his face. "That one hurt, I bet," she said, reaching out to put her hand on his chest. "But the truth is, you're too private for any of those things they say about you to be true."

"I was not a saint, Sam."

"Good, because I've never been a saint, either. Saints are boring. In any case, the past is the past."

"Yeah, thankfully." His hand danced over her skin to her thigh, his thumb making lazy circles on the very inside of that thigh.

Her blood hummed.

She put her hand over the material of her dress, halting his movement because she couldn't take it. "And I can say all this to you, because as I mentioned, we're very alike, you and I."

"I prefer the differences." His first finger stretched out of her hold and barely, just barely, skimmed over her bikini bottoms.

Her entire body jerked, but she wasn't ready to let loose with him, no matter what her hormones were begging. "Do you—"

"Do I...?"

She looked at him. "Ever feel like your life is in a sort of holding pattern? Almost...stalled?"

He went very still, his gaze intent on hers. "Maybe."

"I wonder about it, especially since I met you," she whispered. "Can people outgrow their life? Because I'm just starting to worry that I have."

"Maybe we only outgrow parts of it," he said just as quietly, suddenly as serious as she was. "And maybe new pieces fall into place."

"That's pretty intuitive for a man who doesn't like to think about the future."

"I thought that wasn't a problem for you."

"Oh, it's not. Actually, it's one of the reasons you're so damn attractive," she admitted. "Because this is all very in the moment, very loose and carefree."

He looked at her for a long moment. "Right up your alley, is it?"

"Yep. No pressure, no worries."

"No pressure, no worries," he repeated softly, and smiled. "Then why aren't we jumping each other's bones and calling it a day?"

"Because even women with commitment phobias have their boundaries." She stood up, and smiled down at him. "And one of my boundaries is knowing what I'm getting myself into. Before falling into bed with someone."

"Hey, what you see is what you get," he claimed, but he also stood. She walked to the door, opened it, and hoped like hell he wouldn't touch her again, because if he did, she'd cave faster than a cheap suitcase.

With a sigh, he moved to the door as well. Night had fallen. He eyed it, then her, and then smiled. "Time flies with you."

She looked out into the black sky, a little surprised to find it so.

"I still owe you some basketball lessons," he said. "And in return, I have a favor."

"Hey, I paid for those lessons."

"Relax, this one will amuse you. I want you to teach me to surf."

She gaped at him, then laughed.

"Is that so strange?"

"No, but…" She shook her head. "Why do you want to learn to surf now?"

"Because you do it."

Oh. Oh, how…lovely. "I've been surfing since I could walk, Jack."

"So teach me."

"You're crazy."

He grinned. "But you like crazy."

"I do," she admitted.

"So you'll teach me."

What the hell. "Okay. You teach me some basketball, and I'll teach you to surf." In the spirit of fun, she thrust out her hand for a handshake. "In fact, I'll even go first. Meet me here next weekend. Saturday morning, five-thirty."

"A.M.?"

"A.M."

Jack stared down at her hand, then into her eyes, his slow smile full of wicked intent as he hauled her into his arms and planted a kiss on her that left her head spinning and her body weeping.

"Make it six-thirty," he murmured against her mouth.

"Six." She licked her bottom lip to get the last taste of him. "Or no deal. The surfing's best first thing in the morning."

Another sexy smile, along with a sigh. "Six, then."

Then one more long, hormone-rattling kiss, and by the end of it, her knees were knocking.

"'Night," he whispered.

"'Night."

"Sweet dreams," and he walked out into the night.

Smiling like an idiot, she dreamily watched him go. This was perfect, surface only, fun only, just the way she liked it.

But at the thought, her smile slowly faded.

9

HALFWAY THROUGH the following week, Heather found her brother in his huge backyard, sitting by his oversize pool. She took one look at the surfer magazine in his hands and burst out laughing.

Jack sighed and tossed it aside. "So nice of you to knock."

"If you didn't want me to walk in, you shouldn't have given me a key."

"You could still knock."

"Right. Next time." She plopped down on a lounge chair next to him. "Want to talk about it?"

"It?"

"The brooding look on your face."

"I'm not brooding."

She poked at the surfer magazine. "Maybe we should talk about Sam then."

"What about her?"

"Oh, don't give me that carefully blank look. You like surfer girl and we both know it. She's hot, she's also adorable, though I'm sure she'd hate me saying so."

"Is there a point to this?"

"My point is, I can see why you like her. I like that you like her."

"I don't need your opinion."

Her smile was fond, and she ruffled his hair. "You never have, but when has that stopped me?"

"I just don't want you roping her, or me, or her *and* me, into another event where—"

"Where what? Where you have to have a good time? Where I get to see you smile and look happier than I've seen you since you hung from baskets for a living? Oh, Jack, give up. Give in. Make it easy on yourself. Talk to me."

"You want me to talk to you? Fine. This weekend, she's going to…teach me how to surf."

"That's so sweet. She wants you to be a part of her world."

"I *asked* her to teach me."

"Then that's even sweeter, you wanting to be a part of hers. But you couldn't think of a better way to be with her than risking life and limb? Have you thought about being traditional and going out for pizza and a beer?"

"I don't like traditional."

"You don't *trust* traditional. And why would you? Your professional career was anything but

normal and traditional, Jack. But you have a normal life now." She checked her watch and stood.
"Look, be snide and keep your secrets then. I've
got to run. We're presenting a check for the rec center today at city hall, and—"

"I like her. Okay? I really do." He grabbed her
wrist. "And it scares the shit out of me."

She sank to the chair at his hip and threw her
arms around him. "Oh, Jack—"

"I know. I'm so screwed."

"She'll like you back. She will," she said fiercely.
"Or I'll kill her."

That got a laugh and he peeled her off him.

She leaned in again, kissing him noisily on the
cheek. "I love you, Jack. Now don't go all broody
again, I'm just looking out for you, and in keeping
with that, I'm going to say this with love."

"Oh, boy."

"Listen up, smarty-pants. Stop sulking and go
live your life. Go get her."

"Yeah."

"And, hey, it could be worse. She could be into
skydiving. Or chucking herself off cliffs doing ex-
treme skiing, something like that."

Right. It could be worse.

He'd remember that.

AS THE DAYS PASSED, Sam spent hours on the phone
with Jack, which was strange since she usually hated

the phone. But his voice in her ear made her feel oddly giddy, and she'd hang up wondering how the hell she was supposed to relegate him to just a quickie affair when she liked him so very much.

Saturday dawned clear and beautiful; the sky was tinged pink and lavender. The waves crashed onto the sand with a satisfying thunder that made her anxious to be out there with her board beneath her feet.

She sat on the sand next to Lorissa and Red. Cole was there, too, and Sam hadn't been happy to discover he fit her worst nightmare of a boyfriend for Lorissa. He was beautiful, she'd give him that, all long and rangy and blond, with carefully sculpted muscles that would have been perfectly at home on the cover of *GQ*, but his eyes were cold. When he broke Lorissa's heart—and he would, she was sure of it—she was going to kick his ass, and enjoy it.

She and Lorissa and Red had just done some warm-up stretching. The ocean lapped their feet, and at their backs were their surfboards, standing up in the sand waiting for them.

Sam had an extra board behind her.

"Four- to six-footers," Red said, watching the sets roll in. He wore a one-piece wetsuit hacked off at the knees and shoulders. His long silvery hair was pulled back in a strap of leather.

"So why aren't you out there?" Sam asked. "It's not like you to sit and watch the others."

"I have a feeling this is where the show is today."

Lorissa laughed. She wore surfer shorts and a sunshine-yellow bikini top. "Definitely gotta see this. Cole's brought his camera for blackmail shots."

Cole had wandered off to get some pictures of the surf, so Sam felt free to roll her eyes. "I shouldn't have told you I was teaching Jack how to surf this morning. A camera will send him running."

"Do you really think he'll show?"

"Depends on if she's done the deed with him yet," Red piped in.

"What?" Sam turned her head and glared at him. "What did you just say?"

"It depends on if you—"

"I heard you! I just don't know what that has to do with anything."

"Well, if you haven't, he's still in that wanting-to-please-you stage. He'll be here. Trust me, I know these things."

"And if you *have* been with him—" Lorissa's eyes danced with laughter "—he won't feel the need to get up at the crack of dawn, because pleasing you is no longer necessary."

Sam shook her head. "You guys are sick, and for the record *he* asked *me* to teach him to surf." She heard Jack's SUV roar into the parking lot of the café on the bluff above them and her heart kicked it up a notch.

"She hasn't slept with him yet," Lorissa said to Red, who nodded sagely.

Sam shook her head and got to her feet. "Stay here, both of you. Don't say a word."

Jack appeared at the top of the dune. The light morning breeze ruffled his hair. He wore a light blue hoodie sweatshirt and black swim trunks that came nearly to his knees. As always, no matter where he was or what he was doing—whether in a tux sipping champagne or getting ready to surf for the first time in his life—he looked completely at home.

She knew the exact moment he laid eyes on her because he smiled.

And her heart, still racing, tipped right on its side. She lifted an arm and waved to him, and he began walking down the steps. "What?" she hissed out of the corner of her mouth to Lorissa, who was staring at her.

"Nothing."

"Really? Because that was the most loaded nothing I've ever heard."

"You just waved to him, and jumped up and down at the same time."

They all watched Jack, who had eyes only for Sam, come closer.

"I did not jump up and down," Sam snapped.

"Yeah, you did. Oh, baby, he's got you wrapped," Red said. "And it's quite possible you have him wrapped right back."

"I thought you weren't going to say a word," she said a little unevenly—God, Jack looked good—and started walking to meet him.

Jack's smile spread. "Hey. Sorry I'm a few minutes late. I'm not used to my alarm anymore. Or early mornings."

"No problem." She glanced over her shoulder, eyeing Red and Lorissa with a silent warning to be good. "Jack, you know Lorissa. And this is my uncle, Red."

The two shook hands and Sam looked at Jack. "So are you sure you want to—"

"I'm sure."

"But—"

He set a finger on her lips. "I want to do this. I want to be here. With you."

Okay then. She felt a stupid smile break over her face, and he ran his finger over her lower lip before dropping his hand away. "So…" He eyed the waves and the few surfers out there already doing their thing, and nodded. "Let's go for it."

"Why don't you do a few stretches first?" she suggested. "Save yourself from pulling something."

Once he'd limbered up, she walked him over to

the boards. Both Lorissa and Red still sat there, along with Cole who'd returned from his photo op. Sam didn't look at them.

Jack smiled at Lorissa and Cole. "Aren't you guys going to—"

"Don't talk to them," Sam said. "Or Red. They're all grounded. Grab your board." She pointed to the one she wanted him to take. "Ideally, it should be a foot longer than you, but this is the biggest one I could borrow. It's going to be a couple of inches short but it's wide enough, freshly waxed, and soft-skinned, which is easier to learn on."

"Okay." He carried it to the water's edge.

"How's your knee?"

"Good enough," he said.

Which was probably man-code for it was killing him. Well, she wasn't his mother. "I already know you can swim," she said. "But if you get into trouble, I'll be right there."

He smiled. "I like the sound of that."

God, the way he looked at her. It was lethal to her brain cells. If only he didn't look so hot this morning. He hadn't shaved, and the shadow on his jaw made her want to rub up against him like a cat in heat. "See the leash? You've got to have it around your ankle so you don't inadvertently kill someone. People frown on loose boards out there."

"No loose boards." He nodded agreeably.

She just wanted to toss the boards aside and kiss him. Pathetic. "And the water might appear perfectly calm, but dangerous rips lurk beneath the surface, so watch out. If you get caught in a rip, swim out of it by moving parallel to the shore until you can get in."

"Got it. Anything else?"

"Don't be stupid."

"Got that, too."

She watched as he unzipped his sweatshirt, pulling it off, baring that gorgeous sleek flesh and sinew. His swim trunks were slightly big, which meant they sunk low on his lean hips, revealing a long expanse of rippled belly. "Let's go."

She grabbed her board and started into the water, remembered she still had on her own sweats, and swore. Kicking them off in Lorissa's general smirking direction, she waded in. "Before paddling out, always watch the other surfers to see where it's best to enter the water."

"Yes, ma'am."

She thought he was mocking her but when she looked into his eyes all she saw was a smile, and genuine happiness at being with her. In spite of herself, she grinned back. "Paddling out…lie prone on the board with its nose just above the surface of the water. Use your arms as paddles on either side, like this." She lay on her board and started paddling. "See?"

"Oh, yeah. I see." He was looking at her ass.

"Jack." She laughed. "I mean it."

"So do I. Watch." He tore his gaze off her and easily handled his board.

They paddled side by side. Halfway out, it occurred to her how much she was enjoying herself, and how soon it would all end. It had to, because it always ended—usually by her own doing.

"Hey. You still with me?" Jack reached out and touched her arm. Waited until she looked at him. "If you don't want to do this—"

"No." She sat up on the board and rubbed her temples. Jack sat up, too, while she tried to think, but there were no thoughts to be had other than that this was right and that she wanted to be here. With him. Hanging. Surfing.

"I want to do this. But I also want to do this…" And leaning close, she put her mouth to his.

He reacted immediately, cupping her face with his hand, making a hungry sound of approval deep in his throat that made it hard for Sam to pull away, but she did.

He smiled. "Well, that's a nice start to the day."

Yeah. Very nice. But they were here to get him surfing. She showed him how to study the waves before deciding how far out to paddle. Showed him how to avoid another surfer or swimmer, and how to get into position facing the beach.

"When a suitable wave is coming up on you and there are no other surfers on it, start paddling. When it reaches you, it'll lift you and the board, propelling you forward, so paddle your ass off if it's a wave you want. Take hold of the rails and jump straight to your feet, your front foot about halfway up the board with your rear foot two feet or so behind it and at right angles to the center of the board." She jumped up on hers, showing him. "Make sure that the nose of the board is above the water, not too far up or you'll fall back into the wave and crash, and not too far down or the board'll nose-dive. Got it?"

"Uh…"

"Here, watch." She sank back down, waited for a wave and then showed him how to catch it, how to ride it. Then she paddled back out to where he sat on his board watching. "Ready to try?"

"Is it going to be as easy as you just made it look?"

"Nope."

He laughed. "Well, then, I'm as ready as I'll ever be."

"Okay, when I say go…" She waited until the right exact second. "Go! Paddle!"

Gamely he went for it, and surged his incredibly athletic body up onto the board, leaping to his feet. He waved his hands wildly in the air for the balance that he couldn't seem to find—

And toppled headfirst into the wave.

She winced, but he surfaced just fine. When he paddled back out to her, he offered a humbled smile. "Harder than it looks."

"Want to go back?"

"Nope."

So again she told him when to go, and again he flexed those delicious muscles to stand on the board, to wave his outstretched arms searching for balance—

Only to be taken out by the second crest because it'd taken him too long to get up.

After bobbing up, he tossed his hair back and laughed. "Yeah. Definitely harder than it looks."

When he paddled close again, she reached for his hand and pulled him in so that their legs touched. With him near her, she couldn't keep her hands to herself and she ran them over his wet chest and shoulders.

"What are you doing?" he asked a little hoarsely.

"Making sure you're okay."

His eyes had gone hot. "If I say I'm not, will you keep touching me?"

Laughing, she pushed free, but he snagged her hand and tugged her back to him. "I have an idea," he murmured as they rose and fell with the swells beneath them. "You go for a ride, then let me run my hands all over you." He eyed her wet, clinging black bikini, then without warning hauled her from her board to his lap. "I could really get behind that idea," he said, just before his mouth came down on hers.

Because he tasted so good and felt so big and warm, she sank into him for a long moment, thrilling to his hands gliding over her wet skin, holding her close.

"Stop," she said on a breathless laugh when he had her butt in one hand and his other dancing its way up her rib cage.

"You sure?" His thumb took a lazy skim over her breast.

Hell, no, she wasn't sure. Her body was quivering for his; he could see it, could feel it.

She heard the whooping calls of the other surfers from the shore and knew she'd take a razzing for this. "Jack—"

He smiled into her face before dumping her off his lap. "Stop distracting me. Here comes a good one," and he went, leaving her body still burning from his touch.

It took another couple of hours for him to get it, and she had to hand it to him. He never gave up, even when Red and a couple of his cronies joined them in the water, offering both helpful hints and lots of jokes. But finally he could ride an entire wave in without making any cartwheels off the board or landing facefirst in the sand. Exhausted, he collapsed on the beach.

Sam left Red and the others still in the water and came up next to Jack, lightly slapping him on the butt. "Not bad."

His response was nothing more than a grunt.

"So…I'll see you next weekend."

He cracked open an eye. "Huh?"

"For basketball, remember?"

"Why do we have to wait a week?"

"Because we started out doing the weekend thing, so I figured why ruin a good plan?"

"I need a better reason than that."

How about because she needed a good seven days between viewings of this man—he was far too potent. "Because I don't see you bouncing up to show me anything right now," she came up with brilliantly.

"Oh. Yeah." He closed his eye again. "Right."

"You really didn't do so bad today."

"I guess if I can still hear you, that means I'm still alive." He hadn't moved a muscle.

She ran her gaze down the length of him, more than a little concerned by how much she wanted to throw herself on top of him. Her wants were usually far more controlled than this. "How's the knee?"

"If I say it's awful, will you take me up to your place and make it all better?"

Lorissa, who'd walked over to them with Cole at her side, shook her head with disgust. "And to think I had such high hopes for you."

Still on the sand, Jack rolled over, shaded his eyes from the now-piercing sun and looked up at her. "Too cheesy, huh?"

"Waaaay too cheesy."

"Yeah, you're probably right." With a groan, he stood up, and took Sam's hand. "How's this, instead? Can I take you out to breakfast?"

"Much better line," Cole said. He laughed when Lorissa gave him a baleful stare.

"But it's…lunchtime," Sam said inanely.

"Okay," Jack said, undeterred. "How about lunch?"

"I have to work."

"I'll cover for you," Lorissa offered, but Sam shook her head.

"I'm fine working."

"'Kay." Jack blinked at her innocently. "Then how about some of that lotion for my knee before I go?"

She couldn't refuse him that and he knew it. Before she could think better of it, he'd followed her over the bluffs and up the stairs of the café to her apartment—and into her small bathroom, where his big, tough body crowded her as she reached into her medicine cabinet.

When she turned to hand the lotion to him, he was right there, and putting his hands to her hips, lifted her onto the vanity.

"Jack—"

"Here's the thing," he murmured, his mouth skimming her jaw. "I can't stop thinking about you, about how you taste. Give me another taste, Sam."

He wore only his swim trunks, his chest bare and still damp, his shoulders looking impossibly wide, his head bent in concentration as he nibbled at the corner of her mouth. His hands moved slowly, caressingly, up and down her arms, giving her the same undivided, single-minded attention he'd given to surfing.

She skimmed her hands up his back, rough with sand, and offered him what he wanted, another taste. With a rough groan, his mouth opened hungrily on hers. He dropped the lotion in the sink so his hands could cup her bottom, his fingers flexing against her as she wrapped her legs around his waist, her arms around his neck. "Mmm," rumbled from deep in his throat as he pulled her against the rock-hard bulge now in his swim trunks.

The desire to fall back and let him take her right

there was so strong she nearly pulled off her bikini and sank to her knees on the floor, but instead she pushed free. "I've got things I have to do." She needed some time here, some distance, if for no other reason than to get her breathing back to normal. She'd go make some sandwiches for the café and clear her head. Maybe make herself something extra-fattening for comfort. Reaching behind her, she grabbed the lotion in the sink and put it in his hand. "I'll see you Saturday."

"Chicken," he taunted softly, but he let her hop down and lead him to the front door, which told her he was every bit as much a chicken as she.

OVER THE COURSE of the next week, Sam kept herself busy. She had the café, which was thankfully hopping with late-summer action. She also had her friends, her surfing and any number of things in her life; such as her obsession with making brownies that could be eaten and not used as cement or paint.

But being out in the water only reminded her of the man she dreamed about every night. It didn't help that Lorissa enjoyed asking about him, or that Jack continued to call each evening so they spent long hours on the phone just talking.

By the time Saturday came and she was dressing to meet him, she could hardly stand it.

She was going to sleep with him. Actually, there likely would be no sleeping involved. Just lots of calorie-burning, good sweaty stuff.

Naked stuff.

Oh yeah, naked stuff really worked for her.

And then after that, she'd be over it, over him. She could move on. That's how it always happened, and that's how it would happen here, too. She'd kiss him sweetly and leave.

And never see him again.

It would be mutual, of course; she held no great illusions about herself. She wasn't anything special; in fact, she could be rather difficult, was a natural loner and not at all steady lover material.

Going over all of this in her mind, she drove to Jack's house. He'd called her with directions, and although she'd suggested meeting at a school or a local gym, he'd laughed that off and said he wanted privacy for this.

Privacy. Sounded good to her.

As she neared his place, she wasn't surprised to find herself in an extremely expensive area of Malibu. When she pulled into his driveway and stopped at the gate, she stared at the largest three-story glass-and-concrete beach house she'd ever seen.

She had no idea why it hadn't really occurred to her that Jack Knight was one loaded guy. He probably had more money than she could dream of and more ways to spend it than she could count. Slightly uncomfortable, she pushed the buzzer and waited.

"Hey," came his voice from the speaker. "You look good enough to eat."

She looked into what she'd thought was a mirror next to a number pad but realized it was a camera. She laughed, because she was wearing surfer, not basketball, shorts—she hadn't had any—and two spaghetti-strapped tank tops, one layered over the other. A beat-up old sweatshirt kept her warm in the early morning chill. Not exactly glamorous. She'd found socks at the last moment, and had them tucked into the tennis shoes hanging around her neck. "So do I need a passport to get in or what?"

"Nope, just a smile."

She had that just from the sound of him.

The gate swung open to let her in. She drove up the ambling, curvy driveway toward the house, beyond which was her beloved ocean. She parked right in front of the steps and took in the sight. The property itself—acres and acres of green grass and naturally landscaped beauty—grabbed her by the throat and held on.

She couldn't imagine having this much land to herself, with a private beach, clean of debris and people.

Heaven on earth.

"I'm way out of my league," she whispered and, wondering if he had a butler and a maid and a cook and all that, she turned off the engine.

She firmly reminded herself she was here because they had a connection, a sexual one. It hummed and buzzed in her veins at all times, and it begged to be explored.

She wanted to explore him.

Plus, she'd spent too much damn money on basketball lessons, and the cheapskate in her wouldn't let it go to waste. With all its might, her body hoped learning good basketball meant him having his hands all over her.

A lot.

No matter that her brain maintained that was a very bad idea...

10

JACK JOGGED DOWN his front steps to meet Sam. "Uh-oh," he said, and tugged on her hand until she got out of the car. "You have a certain look on your face."

"Look?"

"Like you can't decide whether to run away or not." He tightened his grip on her fingers. "But I've got you now." He took her tennis shoes—with the rolled-up socks sticking out of them—from around her neck and tucked them under his arm as they started up the steps.

"This place is huge."

"Yeah, I like having lots of room."

"It's the size of a small country."

"Just about." He opened the front door and put his hand on the small of her back, mostly because he wanted to touch her, partly because he wanted to do a hell of a lot more than just touch her. "Ready for some hard work?"

"Work? Is that what basketball is to you?"

"Was." He smiled. "Today, you get to work, and I get to have fun."

She eyed the foyer, which soared to the second floor. "What do you do in here?" She lifted her gaze, studying the huge, open space with all the window lights and fancy glass that lit the place so beautifully. "Play basketball?"

"Nah, I'd break the windows and then my decorator would kill me."

She just looked at him, and he let out a little laugh. "I'm kidding. Well, sort of. Heather decorated this place for me, and now that I think about it, she probably would kill me if I broke something. So do me a favor and don't touch anything."

That made her smile, and he smiled, too. "Much better," he murmured and pulled her in for a hug. "Can't play basketball unless you're smiling. That's the first rule."

She hugged him back. "What's the second?"

"If I said you had to take off all your clothes, would you believe me?"

Laughing, she pulled away. "No such luck."

They walked through a large living room, then the formal dining room he never used and into another open area where there was soft, sink-your-feet carpeting, a big-screen TV, three of the biggest couches on the market and a help-yourself bar. "The great room," he said. "The hang-out room."

She nodded, taking in the warm butter-colored walls filled with pictures and collages of his friends and family and the events in his life. "This is nice."

"Thanks." He pointed to an envelope of photos lying on the coffee table. "Cole was kind enough to take pictures of me falling all over myself learning to surf, and then even kinder to give them to me." Opening the envelope, he flipped through the humiliating shots of him tumbling into the water, being tortured by the waves, and pulled out the one he loved. "This one is going on the wall soon as I get it enlarged."

She stared up at him and then took the picture. "It's of us."

"Yep." It'd been taken after surfing, so he wore only his swimming trunks, and Sam was in that black bikini he had an extremely soft—make that hard—spot for. When Cole had lifted the camera, Sam had started to pull away, but he'd slipped his arm around her. Turning back to him, she'd offered such a sweet, beautifully affectionate smile his heart had melted, and he'd offered her one back. Cole had snapped the shot.

"You're going to put us on your wall with all your friends and family?"

"What, you're not my friend?"

Her mouth shut, and with a frown, she stared down at the picture. "I thought…"

"What?"

She handed him back the picture, and turned her back. "Playing. We're playing. I taught you to surf, now we're going to play ball. Where's the hoop? I'm sure you've got a state-of-the-art one somewhere in here."

So she wanted to go at it like that, like they had nothing going on here, nothing at all. Fine. But suddenly he was far less happy with this no-commitment thing than he'd imagined. "Out here." Through the kitchen, the laundry room and outside to the backyard, where beyond the Olympic-size pool was a basketball court.

She stared at the asphalt, which had cracked last year and now had a few daisies popping up here and there. Then she looked at the regulation-height hoops draped with baskets, one of which had torn in his last fierce battle with some friends. "This is like…street ball."

He grinned broadly. "Yeah. Don't you love it?"

"But…where's the expensive wood floor, the custom paint job, the fancy baskets and hoops?"

He stepped close, tucked a wayward strand of hair behind her ear and then cupped his fingers around her jaw until she looked at him. "I didn't grow up in a house like this, you know. I grew up in a regular neighborhood, playing basketball in the street. I like to play it that way. This way."

"Oh." She smiled, but it slowly faded. "Jack…"

"No." He shook his head. "You're not changing your mind."

She closed her eyes. "I don't want this to end. But if I stay, if we play, we're not going to stop there. And then tomorrow, it'll all be over."

"I'm confused." He ran a finger over her creamy shoulder. "How will it be over?"

"Because I'll be tired of you. I'm always tired of a guy after sex."

He grinned, and shook his head. "But you haven't had sex with me."

"Jack—"

His grin faded. "You're serious. You want to leave now so that we won't have sex and you can keep seeing me."

She nodded miserably.

"We each have a past," he said slowly. "A lot of yours is tragic, and I wish I could change it for you, but as far as past relationships, none of them should factor here. This thing between us is different. Original."

"And scary."

"And scary," he agreed. "But I don't care, and I'm surprised you do."

"What does that mean?"

"It means I thought you had guts and determination and grit, from that first night. I looked at you and saw—"

"A beach bum?"

"A woman I wanted to get to know more, and as I did, I learned how strong you were, what a beautiful outlook you had after that crappy hand Fate dealt you. You played anyway, and won." Stepping close, he put his hands on her arms and ran them slowly up and down as if he could warm her, soften her. Make her see what he saw. "You won. I love that about you, Sam. You live as you are, as you want. Damn, if that isn't one of the hottest things about you. You bid on lessons with me because you wanted it. You wanted me. If you've changed your mind because you've lost your nerve, then I don't know you at all."

That got a rise out of her. "Is that right?"

"Yeah. Now are you in or not?"

She took a long look around and then met his challenging gaze. An ironic smile touched her lips. "You have a way of putting things."

"Don't I?"

"Well, it would be stupid to waste all that money."

He smiled. "Yep."

"Besides…" Now she stepped away from him, rolling her head on her shoulders, warming up. "I'm going to kick your ass."

"I thought this was a lesson."

"How about a game, instead?"

"But…" He had to laugh. "I'm a pro."

"*Ex*-pro." She unzipped her sweatshirt, and let it fall. "And not in street ball."

She wore two tank tops, a light blue one over a white one, both thin enough that her breasts were perfectly outlined. Perfect handfuls.

His palms suddenly itched.

She put on her socks, then took her shoes from him and slipped into them. She stood, her hands on the hips of her surfer shorts, which cracked him up. She lifted a brow. "Bring it on."

"Some fighting words right there."

She let out a slow smile that just about did him in. "Yep."

"Half-court?"

A sound of irritation sounded from her. "Full."

"Single point baskets to five?"

"Eleven. And we'll call our own fouls."

Fouls. So this was going to get rough, was it? "Don't you want a handicap?"

"Well, if you're offering." She shot him a smile that fried his brain cells. "I go to five, you to eleven?"

Her fingers were playing with the tiny little straps on one shoulder, almost nudging them off, and he lost his train of thought.

"Jack?"

"Sure." How hard would it be to beat her? He grabbed a ball from his ball stand, but she snagged it out of his hands and started dribbling down the court away from him.

And then executed the most out-of-step, awkward layup he'd ever seen...and made the shot.

Twirling around she shot him a cocky grin.

He laughed. "I guess we've started."

"Yeah. One zip. Want to up the stakes?"

She was hot as hell, standing on the court with that sexy little smile. He'd probably trip over his own tongue playing her, but she couldn't possibly beat him. "Sure."

"Winner picks their prize."

He was going to trip over his own tongue right this second. "Anything?"

She batted her lashes, and a groaning laugh escaped him because she was teasing him; she couldn't be serious—

"*Anything*," she said.

"You're on." Whether it was taking advantage or not, he would win, and he would claim his prize. In his bed.

"Ready?" She dribbled slowly and easily, making a classic rookie mistake by letting the ball get too far away from her body.

An entire night with her...

The steal was easy, and he jogged down the court away from her, making a layup that would have had any basketball fan sighing in pure pleasure.

Then turned to face her as he tossed her the ball. "One all. Your ball."

SAM TOOK THE BALL and, being the fast study she was, dribbled closer to her body this time, eyeing her opponent carefully. He looked so fierce standing there blocking her, so intense.

He wanted to win, badly. Hmm, Sam thought, wonder what he has in mind for a prize?

The thought made her want to grin, but she held it in. Because she wanted to win, too. Yes, she'd had a moment when she'd wanted to back out and run like hell, but he'd been right. She needed to see this out, at least for the night. She owed that to both of them.

Feigning right, then left, she had to pull back when he didn't give an inch. Twice he reached out and nearly snagged the ball from in front of her nose. He was right, he was a pro. But she had something he didn't, and she planned to use it. Make that "them." She supposed the feminist in her would never ever consider using her breasts to win a basketball game, but she really, really wanted to win.

Backing up a step, she shot him the best come-hither smile she had. Turning in a circle, she ran around him, dropping her left shoulder so that the straps of her tank tops, thin and inconsequential, slipped off.

As Jack passed her and then faced her, blocking her in, she straightened again.

Her breasts, full and unencumbered by a bra, were held in by only the right straps.

Jack didn't miss the show; in fact, he executed an almost comical double take and then tripped over his own two feet. Taking full advantage of that, she took off toward her basket.

And made the shot.

"Foul."

"Was not," she said, and tossed the ball at his chest. "Two one. Your ball."

He eyed her good and long, a sparkle of heat in that gaze that made her want to jump him. He'd begun to sweat, just a little, and he looked like one tall, sinful treat.

She left the two straps hanging down on her biceps.

"So this is how you want to play it," he said very softly.

She just lifted a brow.

"Well, then, understand this. I could look at you all day, and I will, but you're still going down." With that statement, he easily got past her, loped down the court with the confidence of a man not being guarded, and made his shot, a beautifully impressive slam dunk. "Two–two."

She smiled. "Don't take your victory lap yet."

"No?"

"Oh, no." Breasts straining against the thin material of the tank tops, jiggling with her every movement, she dribbled, eyeing him. She could feel the breeze on the exposed skin above the tops, and also below, where she had a good three or four inches of flesh showing between the low slung surfer shorts and the hem of the tanks.

Still dribbling, still smiling, she stopped shifting around and looked right at him. She could tell he was torn between playing the game and lusting after her. He wanted to win, badly, but he wanted to toss the ball away and grab her as well, and it made the amusement drain right out of her as she went into her own lust mode.

When he caught the look in her eyes, he groaned. "You are killing me."

"I plan to," she purred, and blew right by him.

But when she tossed up the ball toward the basket, she missed. She heard him coming after her and grabbed the ball again, putting it back up.

She knew he could have deflected it from going in, but instead he caught her around the waist and hauled her close.

The ball sank in the basket.

"Foul!" she cried anyway, laughing, but again the chuckle faded away when she caught the utter intense, serious, almost terrified look in his eyes. "What?" She put her hand on his chest, feeling his heart pounding beneath her fingers. "Jack? What is it?"

"I don't know. I think it's you."

She let his mouth close on hers, allowing herself to fall into the kiss for a long, wet, deep, hot moment. Then she pulled back and licked her lips. "Three two. My ball." She grabbed it and felt it was a testament to the power of the kiss they'd just shared that she made it all the way to her basket and shot before he even blinked and looked in her direction. "Four two," she said, and smiled. "Game point."

But she'd unleashed the beast with both her actions and that kiss, and for the next few moments he played like…well, like the former NBA superstar he was, racking up the score until it was at nine four.

Damn, he was good. But she had plans for him, and they included him losing so she could claim her prize. Him. All night long. "Man, I'm hot." And with that, she peeled off the light blue tank top, leaving her in just the thin white one.

While his tongue was still hanging out, she made her shot. And missed, damn it.

He came up behind her, making sure his chest and thighs and everything in between brushed against her back when he reached in front of her to commandeer the ball.

With a screech, she hugged it to her chest and ran around him, forgetting to dribble.

"Travel," he called, but she didn't slow down.

She didn't stop until she'd shot. And missed.

"That's what you get for cheating."

She took another shot and made it. With a whoop, she whirled around, doing a little victory dance. "I won."

"Oh, please, you—"

She took another victory dance lap around him, tracing her finger over his damp, gleaming skin as she did.

"—totally cheated—"

She danced backwards, away from him, and scooped up her discarded top. "I'll expect you tonight, Jack."

"You didn't even try to— Huh?" He blinked as her words sank in. "What?"

"I said I'll expect you tonight. I won, not exactly fair and square maybe, but don't worry, I won't cheat you tonight."

"Tonight?"

"Yep." Feeling quite pleased with herself, enjoying the shock and confusion on his gorgeous face, she smiled. "I get to claim the prize," she reminded him gently. "And Jack, my prize is you."

"Me."

"That's right." She laughed at his expression. Poor, poor baby. He hadn't expected to lose. "You. For tonight, our first night. We'll make it count, just in case."

"In case what?"

In case it's also our last. But she just smiled and waved, and took off.

Stunned, Jack could only watch her go. No one had ever walked away from him before. No one.

In fact, it was the first time a woman had wanted absolutely nothing from him—not a promise, not a diamond, not a single damn thing.

Except his body, and quite possibly only for tonight.

Even more unbelievably, that wasn't good enough for him.

JACK PACED most of the afternoon. There was no denying the odd sliver of fear, because he felt this overwhelming pressure to make sure tonight was so good she'd want him again. And again. Because he really didn't think he could walk away from her. He'd walked away plenty of times in the past and never given it another thought.

And, yet, today he thought about little else.

He was determined to change her mind, determined to make her want him as badly as he'd come to want her. He really had no idea how to do that, only that he had to manage it.

That, or be able to say goodbye to her tonight.

Anyone he knew would probably fall over in shock, but the truth was, for the first time in his adult life, he'd become attached to a woman. To the most amazing woman he'd ever met.

Finally, he headed over to Sam's at dusk. He had a bottle of wine under his arm and a foolish hitch in his heart. It should be all about anticipation, and a good amount of it was.

When he pulled into the parking lot, the café was dark, not a single light. She'd closed up.

Perfect.

He opened his door, and an odd scent registered in his brain at the exact moment he saw a plume of smoke coming out the front window of the café.

Squinting, he moved closer. If she'd closed up the café, then there shouldn't be—

Then he saw a flash of orange—a flame—and, with a sinking deep in his belly, started running.

11

SAM'S NOSE twitched at the distinct stench of burning brownies.

Impossible. It hadn't been long enough—only ten minutes or so. She went still and sniffed again, but it was unmistakable now. "Damn it."

She'd had tonight planned down to the last detail. First, bake brilliant brownies, then make herself irresistible-looking and last, but not least, greet that gorgeous hunk of man.

Seduce him.

Then—holding her breath—see what happened afterwards.

Perfect plan.

Until now. She hadn't used her upstairs oven because, besides the timer not working, it didn't cook evenly. Now, she'd just gotten out of the shower and had put on her favorite black lace panties and matching bra when the smell had reached her. With a groan, she grabbed her old, ratty, favorite bathrobe and started running down the stairs.

But when she tore into the café kitchen, her robe flying out behind her, she skidded to a halt and stared at the oven in horror.

She hadn't burned the brownies; her oven had. Flames licked at them from beneath, curled round the edges of the stove, and licked the cabinets on either side.

"Damn, damn." Whirling, she headed to the counter, and the phone. Yanking up the receiver, she dialed 911, then put the phone in the crook of her neck and spun around again, this time toward the closet, and the fire extinguisher she kept there.

She couldn't believe how hot it'd gotten already, and she glanced over her shoulder, nearly screaming as the dispatcher answered, because the fire was right there, right in front of her now, where it hadn't been seconds ago.

A window exploded, and she dropped to the floor. "Oh God, oh God." Tripping over her robe, she fumbled with the extinguisher. But flames leaped to the ceiling, and suddenly the rest of the cabinets had caught fire. So had the counter. "Got a kitchen fire," she yelled into the phone, and gave the address.

The dispatcher took the info with quick professionalism. "Ma'am, I hear the flames. You're too close."

"I'm leaving right now." As soon as she figured out exactly how to do that.

"The trucks are on their way."

"They'd better hurry."

"They are," he assured her. "Are you outside yet?"

"Going."

"Seriously, ma'am. Don't try to save anything but yourself."

She wasn't stupid, she knew better. But it wasn't just smoke clogging her throat and making her hesitate as she took a good look around. So much of her life was here, right here. And before her very eyes it was going…

"No." But the place was beyond her help, she knew that. "Out," she reminded herself, wincing because the heat was searing her skin as she stood there. With the extinguisher, she spurted the fire directly in front of her to make a path. Smoke rose, choking her, but it worked. All she had to do was duck under the counter—burning now—and she'd have a clear shot at the door.

She used the extinguisher again, and dropping on all fours, started crawling under the counter, a task made more difficult because of her long robe, but finally she was past the flames enough to stand up in the dining area.

Weaving a little unsteadily, she looked back at

the kitchen that had been her life for so long, and her heart lurched.

Her entire life…

Behind her, something crashed, startling her. Whipping around, she saw Jack straighten from where he'd kicked down the door. He started toward her, his expression filled with horror and fear.

All that strength, she thought fuzzily. She'd definitely had different plans for those muscles tonight.

He grabbed her, pulled her hard to him, lifting her face to his. "Sam—"

"The brownies burned." She felt a sob rise. "All of them."

He started to say something, but she couldn't hear over the shattering of another window behind her. Jack shielded her body with his while glass rained down, mingling with the falling ash and thick smoke. "Out," he yelled. "Now."

The next thing she knew they were standing in the parking lot, in the warm night, staring back at Wild Cherries as the entire building went up in flames and smoke.

She blinked up at him. Had he carried her, or had she walked? She looked down at her bare feet, streaked with dirt, and couldn't remember.

The fire lit up the night sky, the noise hurt her ears. Urgently, Jack put his hands on her arms. "Are you hurt? Are you burned? Where?"

Her hands were fisted as she took in the sight of her life burning. She shook her head and felt the tears in her throat, which surprised her because she never cried, never even felt like crying, but another glance at the blazing building behind them reminded her she hadn't had a big loss in a while, either. At least nothing that had mattered.

This mattered. God, this really mattered. "I probably should have grabbed some clothes."

"Sam, look at me." His voice was low, insistent and filled with fear, which brought her back.

Her palm stung, and she figured she'd cut it, but she kept her hands closed because the thing that hurt the most was her heart. "I'm okay."

"We're shaking. Let's sit." He pulled her down on the curb.

"Here they come," she said when sirens sounded from down the road.

"Yes. Sam, sweetheart, look at me. Let me see your eyes."

"It's going to be too late, you know."

"It's not too late, you're still breathing." He hugged her tight. "When I pulled up and saw the flames—" A breath stuttered through him.

"You were scared."

"Try terrified."

She stared at him, feeling like her entire heart

sat in her mouth. "How did this happen between us, Jack? It's too fast, we've only—"

"Shh." He held her again, and this time she leaned her head on his shoulder. "It's going to be okay."

No. No, it wasn't. "I had quite a night planned," she murmured, gripping his shirt in her fists. "I was going to seduce you in black lace and then I was going to do it again, just because."

"I'll take a rain check." He stroked a hand down her back and rubbed his cheek over her hair. "But trust me, the black lace would have worked as many times as you had it in you."

She let out a sobbing laugh and held on tight, closing her eyes to the sight of flames leaping into the night.

Two fire department engines roared into the parking lot, but the old building had already taken too much of a beating.

Face blank, Sam watched the fight, only her eyes reflecting her emotions, and Jack had never felt so helpless as he did right then watching her watch her life go up in smoke.

She'd suffered so many damn losses; this was just another in a long string of them, and he could hardly stand it. He wanted to shove his wallet at her, wanted to buy her the moon, if only to take away the hollow devastation etched so clearly in her green eyes. But that wouldn't work here. He couldn't fix this for her.

She'd had her fists clenched and he reached for one now, holding it between his hands. "Sam—" He'd been about to try to get her to sit again, but frowning, he looked down at her sticky hand. It was dark but he could still see the even darker stain dribbling from her fingers.

His heart caught. "Sam, open your hand."

She did, then gasped in pain. Her palm had been sliced, probably on glass when she'd crawled out of the kitchen.

"Here." Jack cradled her hand in his while he gently probed for slivers, her every sharp, pained breath stabbing into him. "It's clean," he said with some relief and pulled off his shirt, turning it inside out for the cleanest area, then pressing it to her hand to try to stanch the blood.

Around them, it seemed as if the firefighters had put out the fire nearly as fast as it'd started. And then the questions began. Sam told them everything she could in a flat voice and with an even expression that worried Jack to the bone.

Too calm, he thought. She was way too calm.

"Is it all gone then?" she asked them in a carefully neutral voice. "Is there nothing to save?"

"Not sure what the cap'll say," the firefighter

told her. "But it looks like you might have some of the base framing left."

Eyes unreadable, she nodded.

And Jack's own burned for her.

The ambulance arrived. Sam turned to Jack, face streaked with dirt and ash, bathrobe torn and grubby, and said, "I don't want to go to the hospital."

"Sam—"

"I'm okay."

She needed stitches, and one look at the paramedic's face verified that. "I'll come with you," he said. "But you're going."

NINE STITCHES LATER, Jack put Sam back into his SUV. He'd had plenty of stitches in his time and broken bones as well, not to mention three surgeries; but he'd never been on the holding-the-hand side of things. When they'd put a needle into Sam's wound, he'd actually seen stars, but hadn't allowed himself to look away.

"Breathe, Knight," she'd said dryly, and he'd taken a shaky breath to keep from passing out.

Some hand-holder.

Now she sat in his car, wearing her now grungy robe, beneath which was the black lace lingerie he had a few glimpses of and was having a hard time keeping his mind off of, even now. Wearily, she set her head back on the seat. "Stop worrying," she said, eyes closed. "I'm fine."

"I'm not worrying," he said. Much.

"I need to call Lorissa and Red. One of them will let me use a couch. It wouldn't be the first time."

"No."

Craning just her neck without moving another inch of her body, as if she were so exhausted she couldn't manage it, she looked at him.

"My house," he said.

Giving in much easier than he expected, she nodded. "Your house."

She sounded defeated, which was so out of character, even given the events of the night, that he wondered how much pain she was in—she'd refused to take the meds offered her at the hospital. Figuring he'd bully her into taking them at home, he concentrated on the drive.

Twenty minutes later when he pulled up his driveway and turned off the engine, she hadn't said another word. For a moment, he just looked at her, lying so still against the seat, eyes closed, injured hand cradled in her good one.

"Sam." He put his hand beneath hers. "I'm so sorry."

"It's not your fault."

"Yeah, but it's not yours, either," he said, knowing he'd gone to the crux of her thoughts when she grimaced. He got out of the car and came around for her, but she slipped out and stood before he got there, then grumbled when he scooped her up.

"Put me down. I hurt my hand, not my feet."

He strode to the front door with her in his arms.

"Jack, don't be stupid, you'll hurt your knee." She rolled her eyes at him when he propped her up between his body and the door while he fumbled for his keys. "What, no butler?"

"When I thought you were going to be taking advantage of me all night, I gave him the evening off."

"Let me walk, Jack. You're acting like a he-man."

He sighed. "Maybe you could lean on someone, just for tonight. Lean on me, Sam."

Her eyes drifted closed, and she snaked her arms around his neck. "I suppose I could…just for tonight."

"Tonight," he agreed grimly, wishing he'd asked for longer.

He carried her upstairs, setting her down in his bathroom, next to the large whirlpool tub. "Bath?"

"Yeah." She watched him turn on the water and test the temperature. "I can take it from here."

"'Kay." He stroked his fingers down her jaw. "Call me if you need anything."

He paced the house for a while. When he came back into his bedroom, she was sitting in the middle of his bed wrapped in two of his towels, looking a little lost. He went into the bathroom, filled a glass with water and brought it to her. "Here." He pulled out the bottle of pills and shook two into her hand. "Take 'em."

"I'm fine."

"Take them anyway."

That she did spoke volumes. "I'll be listening for you," he said. The towels revealed the mile-long legs he'd hoped to have wrapped around him all night long. "If you need anything, anything at all, call for me, okay?"

"Sure."

Ah, hell, there was a quiver in her voice, and his feet stopped moving, stopped taking him farther away and drew him back to the bed. "Sam…"

"No." Her voice was a bare whisper as she pulled her feet in, tucking them beneath her so that she was just a little ball. "I'm fine. Really."

But that was a lie, and they both knew it. He sat on the bed and put a hand on her thigh. Beneath the terry cloth, she was shaking. "Oh, Sam…"

"I'm fine," she repeated, but covered her face.

"Can I do something?" he asked gently. "Make you something to eat?"

"Jack." She managed a mirthless laugh. "You're hovering."

"I know, damn it." He ran his hand up and down her leg as if he could warm her up when he knew that wasn't why she shook—it was from lingering shock or just utter desolation. "I'm feeling pretty helpless here, and I don't do well with helpless."

"Then stop it. Just…go away."

"I thought I could, but no can do." Scooping her into his lap, he leaned back against the headboard. "Tell me what to do, Sam. Tell me, and I'll do it."

She shook her head and looked away, but not before he saw her eyes go glossy with unshed tears. And just like that, he was a goner. "Please." He put his forehead to hers. "You're breaking my heart. Do something. Yell, scream, cry, have a fit…you're entitled."

"All right." With her eyes closed, she slid her one good hand around his shoulders and pressed her face in the crook of his neck. When she squirmed a little to make the fit even tighter between them, her bottom ground lightly into his lap.

"Sam—"

"This." She bit his neck, then soothed it when a kiss. She lifted her face, lightly cupping his with her bandaged hand. "This is what I want." Fumbling between them, she opened the towels, revealing the tanned, subtle skin and sweet curves he'd been dreaming about for weeks now.

A natural blonde, he thought, and closed his eyes on another groan.

"Oblivion," she said in a barely there voice, shifting in his lap restlessly.

Yeah, oblivion worked for him, too, but he couldn't take advantage—

"I want it from you."

"Sam—"

She rubbed that mind-blowing body against his, making him shake with the effort to hold back.

"Wait. Listen." He struggled for thought, not easy when it wasn't his brain in charge at the moment. He had to close his eyes to block the vision of that glorious body sprawled over his, but even that didn't help because she was imprinted in his mind. "You're in shock. You're sick with it." He sounded desperate, even to his own ears. "You have stitches in your hand for crissake. We can't—"

"Take me, Jack. "

"Sam—"

"Make me forget. Please?" And to seal the deal, she put her mouth on his.

12

SAM CONCENTRATED on the feel of Jack's arms around her, of the protective, tender way he held her tightly to him.

Nothing mattered right this second except this, and to prove it, she danced her tongue to his, inhaling the low, rough male sound he made, the one that was so sexy in its neediness that she deepened the kiss even more just to hear it again.

He didn't disappoint.

Yeah, she needed this. She needed his strength, his passion, the way she felt when his arms banded even more tightly around her.

She held him close, her lips clinging to his while her good hand smoothed its way down his chest, tugging his shirt from the waistband of his jeans, then gliding beneath to touch that hot flesh and sleek muscle.

Releasing her long enough to whip off his shirt, he wrapped her back in his arms. "Your hand—"

"Doesn't hurt." She arched into him, pushing

him flat to the bed, sprawling over the top of him. He hissed out an oath, a low, desperation behind it that only egged her on. With her left hand she went for the buttons on his Levi's. "I'm not fragile, I'm not going to break." Pop went his first button.

Pop. Pop.

Again he swore, then ran his hands down her arms to her wrists. Gently flipping her onto her back, he brought her arms up over her head, holding them pinned to the pillow above her, achingly careful with her bandaged hand. "Sam." His chest rose and fell with each harsh breath. "Hold still a sec. I can't think when you—"

"I don't want to think." She tugged at his hold and with a worried grunt, he let her go.

"Be careful," he said. "You—"

"You're not listening…I'm not going to break, I promise." She tossed back her head. She knew her eyes were filled with pride and the heart-wrenching sorrow of the night, but she had to have this. *Him.* She knew she should be shocked by her need, disturbed by her lack of modesty, but she wasn't. "If you don't want me, just say so."

His expression was incredulous. "Are you kidding?" His gaze swept over her, and with the towels discarded, she lay there open and utterly defenseless to him. Slowly he lowered himself over her, covering her with his body, spreading her legs to accommodate his. He cupped her face. Then he kissed her deeply, his hips grinding slowly, purposely to hers, and she felt him, hard and heavy against her. "Feel that?" he murmured.

Oh, yes. Yes, she did, and because of it, pleasure and need entwined, coiled…bordered on frustration.

"Feel how much I want you," he breathed, his mouth against hers.

Sheer desire had her arching her back a little to feel even more of him. "Do you have a condom?"

Reaching out, he opened a drawer in the nightstand by the bed. There was a strip of them there, and he tore one off and held it up. Then he tossed the towels to the floor. Feeling shameless, she sprawled out a little, watching him. Needing him.

He stood up, his shirt already gone, his Levi's undone, and stripped himself down to skin and muscle, and oh my, what skin and muscle he had! Quite simply, the long hard lines of limbs, his tight, corrugated belly, his powerful thighs and everything between them took her breath. She couldn't tear her eyes off of him.

He lay down beside her again. Cupping a breast, he kissed the peak, then pulled back and caressed it with his thumb. "You're so beautiful, Sam."

"Not like you." His virile nakedness made it

difficult to breathe. She wanted to touch and taste. She wanted everything.

He let out a rough laugh. "A woman's body has got it all over a man's. There's so much to look at…" He stroked the backs of his fingers over her breasts and watched intently while the sensitive tips puckered tight for him. "So much to touch."

She felt the tug of his caress now, of his fingers, his mouth, all the way to her womb. She was melting, dissolving away in pleasure.

He swirled his tongue around a nipple, then lifted his head to watch it contract even more. He did it again and again, before finally sucking her into his mouth.

She couldn't help it; she cried out and thrust against him. And he merely started over with her other breast while his hand slid down her belly. His fingers slipped toward her moist curls. Her body responded to the sharp, burning electrical current, her every nerve leaped with anticipation, driving need…

His hand dipped a fraction lower, but not nearly low enough.

"Jack." She wrapped her fingers around his erection, and got even more excited when he swore roughly. Then his mouth had claimed hers again, hungrily, greedily.

But still he didn't take her, still he held back.

"I'm not hurting," she promised, panting from his kisses, his touches. "Don't hold back."

"I don't intend to." He set a big hand on her knee, urged her legs even further apart, then lowered himself between her thighs. With his shoulders wedging her legs open, she was fully exposed to him. He ducked his head.

For a moment, she was too shocked at the unexpected move to do more than let out a squeak, and then in the next moment she was a slave to his tongue. The fingers of her good hand slid into his hair, fisted. The sounds that tore from her throat might have shocked her in their neediness if she could think, but she couldn't. She could only react.

And when her climax came, it dazed her, pummeled her. She was gasping for breath, her skin shining with perspiration, hair clinging to her neck and face. A wreck. A total wreck.

And loving it.

His skin was damp, too, and he levered himself up, face tight, eyes on hers, arm quaking faintly where he held himself rigid over her as he slipped on the condom. She watched, unable to tear her eyes off his hands as they glided the sheath down the most impressive erection she'd ever seen. She'd thought the whole event was pretty much over for her after her own orgasm, but then Jack guided himself home and sank into her to the hilt.

It was a tight fit. Eyes closed, face contorted in a mask of immense pleasure, he gripped her hips and rolled his, making them both gasp at the way her wet flesh gripped him.

With his name on her lips, she held on to him, digging her fingers into his biceps, having never before experienced anything as intense, as overwhelmingly earth-shattering in her life.

Jack kept up with the unerring, slow grinding of his hips, forward and back, forward and back, each thrust bringing her to a new height. Giving herself completely over to it, to him, Sam fought to keep her glazed eyes open and on his, but it was an effort.

Tilting up her hips, Jack sank more fully into her, each subsequent slow withdrawal followed by a desperately craved thrust. Whether it was her panting his name, or his own driving need, he gradually increased the tempo, until unbelievably, she could feel herself spiraling again, shuddering with her second orgasm. As she fell, he rasped out her name and followed her over the edge.

JACK CAME TO HIS senses with great effort. Lifting his weight off of Sam, he was surprised when she murmured a soft *no* and pulled him back down on top of her.

"I'm too heavy." But he stayed an extra minute anyway, brushing a kiss at her temple, and then, when he managed to hoist up his body again, dropped another gently, just between her lovely breasts.

When he came back from the bathroom, she was exactly where he'd left her, eyes closed, a small smile playing around her lips. That it widened when he approached the bed told him what he wanted to know, what he'd hoped to know.

She still wanted him.

She lifted her arms and, not realizing he'd been standing there holding his breath, he let it out and climbed back on the bed.

Pulling the blankets up over them, he lay on his side facing her and hauled her close. She tipped up her head and sought his mouth. With a groan, he sank into the kiss that was every bit as hot and sweet and deep as what they'd just shared. "Sam," he gasped when her hand wandered down his chest, past his belly to wrap around the part of him that was ready for her again. "You need—"

"This," she said simply, and pressed against him, fitting there so perfectly that his response was far more than physical.

That shocked him for a moment, the realization at how right this felt, how much he liked having her in his bed.

It shouldn't have made sense. He hadn't wanted a woman in his life, had thought he didn't have room for one, but this all seemed right.

Since that was as terrifying as dragging her out of the fire, he shoved it aside and dived into what she was offering. He kissed her until she was panting softly, writhing against him again, until he didn't know where she ended and he began. The little sounds in the back of her throat were an unbearable turn-on; so was the way she tore free and demanded, "Another condom," then climbed over him to get it out of the drawer herself.

She tried to open the packet, but couldn't seem to manage with her bandaged hand, so he took it from her. As he ripped the package, she shot him a smile that sent his thoughts reeling. God, he wanted to please her, make her forget, make her his.

But then with her good hand, she pushed him onto his back on the bed.

"Sam—"

"I'll be careful," she promised, then straddled his hips, looking down at him with darkly slumberous eyes. "Very careful."

He groaned, his hands coming up to her hips, then skimming to her breasts, which he plumped up, loving the way her nipples reacted to his touch as she slowly sank down on him.

She bent low, kissing him, her hair brushing his

face, his chest, her body soft and wet for him. Bowled over, he could only hold on. "My God, Sam…"

"I know. It's beautiful. You're beautiful," she said, and then she began to move, slowly, entwining the fingers of her good hand in his, up by his head.

Helplessly, he rocked his hips, and she gasped at the depth he reached inside her.

There was no holding back—he was hers.

Just as, for this moment at least, she was his. Lust might have powered this act, but lust couldn't sustain it alone. His growing, unnamed feelings for her did that.

Flushed, skin damp and glowing, she tossed her head back in pure abandonment.

Pleasured as he'd never been before, he pushed up high inside her. Stroke for stroke his hips met hers, the friction and tension building to unbearable heights, and then she cried out again, lost. And he was lost, too, just from watching her. Hell, he'd been lost in her since that very first night, so much so that he couldn't have held back if he tried. So he didn't, and pulling her down on him, held her tight as he followed her into that oblivion she'd wanted, knowing it was only there, in his deepest thoughts, that he could really make her his for keeps.

13

SAM LAY IN the dark. She was cushioned by Jack's bed and his body, which was wrapped around her. The clock glowing by the bed said twelve-fifteen.

She felt as if she'd lived five years since the fire, but it had only been a few hours. She knew Jack had waited, awake in the dark, stroking her softly, until she'd drifted off, before finally allowing himself to fall asleep.

She'd faked it. Sleep, that is. There'd been no reason to fake anything else with the man, certainly not anything in the sexual department. She'd already known he could be crazily enthusiastic when it came to basketball, or learning new things, or Heather's charity—and now she knew he was as wildly passionate in bed as well.

Jack Knight had treated her body like a temple, worshipping her into a limp noodle. Even with the crushing sadness and despondence of losing Wild Cherries, she knew that she'd shared something different with Jack. Something deeper.

Soul deeper.

That would probably terrify her later. But for now, she could only see the flames, feel the smoke choking her lungs and remember what her home had looked like as they'd driven away.

Throat tight, she slipped out of bed. She grabbed whatever piece of clothing she could find on the floor, which turned out to be Jack's shirt, and slipped into it, then found her way to the massive kitchen and the phone on the wall. Sitting on a bar stool, she lifted the receiver and dialed Red's number.

He didn't answer, so she left a message. "I messed up really good this time. Nothing as simple as a call to the principal or a trip to the police station is going to get me out of this one." Her voice thickened. "I burned your place down, Red. I know you won't be surprised, I was bound to screw up sooner or later." Her voice cracked and she bit down on her lower lip. "I'm so sorry. I'll meet you there in the morning."

She hung up and stared at the phone, her vision blurry. Damn it, she wasn't going to cry now. She dialed again. "Lorissa."

"'Lo," came her friend's sleepy voice.

"I'm sorry to wake you…"

"Sam? Hey, hon, what's up?" Muffling the receiver, Lorissa murmured something out of range, and Sam heard Cole's low reply. Lorissa came back on the phone with an apologetic laugh. "I'm sorry. You caught me in the middle of—"

"Wild Cherries is gone."

Lorissa stopped laughing and the sleepiness disappeared from her voice. After all they'd each been through in their lives, separately and together, neither of them ever joked about things like this, ever. Sam heard her say, "Cole, baby, I need a moment." Then she was back. "What do you mean gone?"

"Burned. To the ground. Or at least I think it is. It was looking pretty shaky when I saw it last."

"Oh my God. Where are you, are you okay, what happened—?"

"I'm at Jack's now, and I'm fine. More or less."

"More or less? What does that mean?" Panic and fear filled her voice. "I'll be right there—"

"No, really. I'm okay." Sam looked down at her bandaged hand, which was beginning to throb like a son of a bitch. "Just a few stitches in my hand, that's all. Lorissa, we're both out of a steady job."

"Hey, we've been poor before."

Sam leant on the countertop and closed her eyes. The adrenaline was finished. The sexual excitement was gone. And she was left with nothing but a bone-deep weariness. "But this time, it's bad. I have nothing. Nothing left."

"Honey, being jobless, that we can manage. Homeless, too. You know you'll stay with me. But being without you…nope. No can do. So I figure everything is damn good. Now tell me where Jack lives, I'll be right over—"

"I'll be okay but can I meet you at the café in the morning?"

Lorissa was quiet a moment. "Is he taking good care of you then?"

Sam felt a hand settle on her shoulder, a big, warm, comforting hand, and her eyes filled. Was he taking good care of her? He'd held her hand in the ER, even after turning an entertaining shade of green when they'd brought out the needles. He'd carried her into his house, given her his bed and then had caved when she'd thrown herself at him, loving her body and soul into the oblivion she'd asked for. "Yeah. He is." Her voice trembled. She still didn't look at Jack, standing behind her, using two hands now to massage the tightness out of her neck and shoulders, moving his fingers in a soothing, circular motion, up and down her spine. "I'll see you in the morning."

"You promise you're okay?"

"I promise I will be."

"Oh, Sam." Lorissa started to cry. "I love you."

She bit back her sob. "Love you, too." Reaching out, she hung up the phone, but kept her head down. "Sorry," she managed to Jack. "Didn't mean to wake you."

"You didn't." With his long fingers, he scooped her hair out of his way, baring her neck to him. "I knew you weren't sleeping. I was just trying to give you your space."

That was so unexpectedly sweet, she felt a tear break loose. She kept her head down until she thought she could control her emotions. "Thanks."

Again he stroked his hand over her back. "I think you've had enough space, Sam."

Lifting her head, she turned on the bar stool so that she could face him. He'd pulled on a pair of sweat bottoms and nothing else. In the harsh glare of the kitchen light, his hair stuck straight up— probably from her own fingers. He had a five o'clock shadow on his jaw, and his shoulder sported a red mark that looked suspiciously teeth-shaped—her teeth.

He looked sexy as hell, and she wanted him again. Standing, she slipped her arms around his waist and leaned her head against him. "You're right. I don't want any more space. Not for the rest of the night. Take me back to bed, Jack."

"Your hand—"

"Will be fine, as long as you've got yours on me." She sighed when he scooped her up against his warm, hard chest. "I guess I need to reconsider this he-man thing. I think I like it." Her arms slipped around his neck. "I like it a lot."

Back in his bedroom, he set her on the rumpled bed. The only light came from the hallway, slanting shadows across the room as he lowered himself over her, bridging her body with his arms. He stroked the lone tear from her cheek. "I don't suppose you'd take a pain pill and get some rest."

She ran her hands up his bare, sleek back, then down again, slipping them beneath his low slung sweats to hold on to the sweetest, hardest male buns she'd ever seen.

A low laugh escaped him as he cupped her face and moved his hips against hers. "Okay, so you're not ready to sleep, yet."

"Don't tell me you are." A little moan escaped her when he rolled his hips again, his body unmistakably responding to their play. "Oh, goodie."

"And this time when we're done," he murmured softly, dropping a sweet, clinging kiss on her lips, "if you still can't sleep, you'll tell me."

"I don't want to keep you up all night."

"You'll tell me," he said firmly, kissing her again, then lifting his head and looking into her eyes. "And I'll keep you company until you can."

"What will we do?"

"Whatever you want."

"Jack—"

Again he lowered his mouth to hers, and she met him halfway. It was what she wanted, the mindlessness of it, the easy release. Hot, fast, sweaty sex—just what the doctor should have ordered.

Only it was as if he already knew her too well because he changed tactics on her, giving her the one thing she couldn't resist, or hide behind. Gentleness. Tenderness. An unfathomable soul-wrenching connection, lingering over her mind and spirit, until she was practically sobbing with it.

He took her where she'd never been before, something that would have terrified her, if she hadn't sensed he was right there with her, just as lost, just as terrified. And by the time it was over, and they lay gasping and panting in each other's arms, she knew she was also fulfilled, another thing she'd never experienced before.

SAM WOKE UP in the arms of a big, warm, naked man, which was a great way to start the day.

Unless you'd burned your home and place of work to the ground the night before. Just as quickly, her euphoria died, replaced by a gut-crushing despondence. *My God, it had really happened—*

Jack's eyes opened, and in their sleepy depths was sorrow for her as he stroked her hair from her face. It was a gesture that tugged even further on a heart that felt as if it had cracked open last night.

God, this man. He had a way of making her melt. He was so wonderful, so hot, so sexy…and so not her future.

They'd already agreed on that.

Only problem, she no longer even knew what her future *did* hold. All she knew was that she had to go see Wild Cherries by daylight. Had to go take an assessment and make some decisions.

Her heart squeezed, but she slipped out of his arms and got out of bed. "I've got to go."

He bent an elbow and propped his head up with his hand, lying in that great big bed looking like one great sexy temptation. "Why don't you let me make you breakfast first?"

She walked toward the bathroom. She picked up her panties and pulled them on. "You really know how to cook in that fancy kitchen?"

"Why don't you stay and find out?"

There was her bra, beneath her discarded robe. Straightening, she began to put in on. "I can't. I want to get to the café."

With a sigh, Jack roused himself out of bed. His two feet hit the floor and then he rose, quite impressive in all his morning glory. "I'll drive you."

"I can call a cab—"

"I'm driving you." He came close, cupped his

hands to her face and tilted it up to his. "Did you really think I'd let you do this alone? Face it in the light of day all by yourself?"

Damn it, her eyes stung again, and she tried to turn away but he held her in a gentle grip of steel. "I'm sticking," he said in a voice that had as much strength as his hold. "We do this together."

"Lorissa is going to meet me there. Red, too. I'll be fine."

"Sam—"

"I don't need a baby-sitter, Jack."

"Yeah. I can see that." He looked her over for a long moment, then dropped his hands.

She turned away from him because she couldn't handle the emotion he stirred within her. She also couldn't handle putting on her dirty bathrobe, and picked up his sweats and T-shirt. "Can I—"

"Anything."

Nodding, she pulled on his clothes, rolling the waist of the sweats to her hips so they'd fit better, and tying his shirt at her waist. Then she turned and faced his hurt silence. "It's not like we are each other's futures, Jack. We talked about that, on day one. We're not, we know we're not."

Again he just looked at her for a long moment, then went to his dresser for clothes for himself. "Sometimes, Sam, things change, even when you don't want them to."

She went utterly still. Could he possibly believe that? Or was that just a certain body part talking? Because in her experience, thinking ahead never mattered, things happened. And they never happened as planned. The word *future*, and all it entailed, was just a slippery, untenable dream. "My future is a charred black pit. And I need to get to it."

He fastened his Levi's. Grabbed a clean shirt and pulled it over his head. Looked at her.

And the message in his eyes nearly brought her to her knees.

He had feelings for her, she didn't doubt that. Hell, she had feelings for him, too—big, scary, gargantuan feelings that would probably overwhelm her if she didn't already have the fire to deal with.

"It doesn't have to be so cut-and-dried," he said very quietly.

Oh, yes, it did. Otherwise, she could get quite accustomed to his beautiful face and those eyes looking inside her, deep inside, to the real Samantha O'Ryan. With no effort at all, she could fall hard, she thought, and rubbed the physical ache spreading beneath her ribs. For the first time in her life, she could really tumble, and the joke would be on her.

Because he wouldn't fall, not for her.

Are you sure? asked a hopeful little voice deep inside. *Are you sure he wouldn't?*

Of course he wouldn't. They weren't even in the same league. He was wonderful, and for now thoroughly engaged with her, but that wouldn't last. No, for both of them, this was nothing more than a quick fling, beautiful and hot, but coming to an end.

Better not to take the plunge at all, than to land on her face in the mud.

Lorissa had taught her that years and years ago after her own disastrous attempt at love had failed so badly, and Sam had taken that mantra to heart. She managed a smile, even though she knew it was a sad one.

"Sam—"

"Please," she said, her smile faltering at the expression in his eyes. "Let's just go."

Looking extremely conflicted and unhappy, he nodded. "Fine. But after, we talk."

No, after, she'd go off and lick her wounds, all of them, alone. That's how she did things, and that's how it worked best.

14

THEY HIT TRAFFIC on the highway. Not unusual by any means, but Sam nearly bit all her nails to stubs on the drive. Twice Jack tried to talk to her, but she just shook her head, unable to hold a conversation, unable to think until she saw for herself.

Maybe somehow it wasn't as bad as she remembered. Maybe, by some miracle, they'd been able to save—

No. She could see the building as they came down the street, or what was left of it—a shell of what it had once been. A blackened, charred shell.

The parking lot was cordoned off. The fire inspector's truck was parked just on the inside of the yellow tape blocking their way in. Jack slowed his SUV to a stop, forced to wait for a break in the traffic before he could turn around and park on the street.

Unable to sit still, Sam hopped out. She heard Jack swear, heard him call out for her, but she didn't slow down. Couldn't slow down. There were just some things that she had to do alone, and this was one of them.

Ducking under the caution tape, she ran toward the burned building, passing the tall proud sign she'd once painted that still read Wild Cherries. Ironically, it wasn't even singed.

Sam eased up and walked toward the only real home she'd known since eighth grade. Behind the charred mess, the ocean churned and pounded the shore, as always. A few early beach goers walked along the edge of the breaking surf, as always.

But she wouldn't be opening the doors of the café today. She wouldn't be having fun creating interesting and delicious sandwiches. She wouldn't go upstairs into her apartment and be at home there.

It just occurred to her. Her surfboard was gone. Her toothbrush. Her favorite pajamas. The photo album of her parents.

All gone.

Her heart tightened. This loss is nothing, she assured herself. Nothing like her other losses. She could start over, find a new place, buy a new toothbrush.

She couldn't buy a new life. She was lucky. Although her heart was breaking, she told herself this with each step that brought her closer and closer to the charred building.

She would have stepped inside—inside being

a relative term now the roof was gone—but a man blocked her way. The patch on his left pec proclaimed him Fire Inspector. He had a clipboard in his hand and a kind look on his face that for some stupid reason made her catch her breath.

If he so much as asked her if she was okay, she was going to lose it.

"Is this your place?" he asked, and when she nodded jerkily—all she could give him—he sighed. "I'm Timothy Adams, Fire Inspector."

"Samantha O'Ryan."

"I'm sorry, Ms. O'Ryan, but this building is a complete loss."

She swallowed hard and stared at her empty, empty building. "Surely something's left."

"Possibly. But you can't go inside just yet, not until it's cleared."

"But—"

"I know how difficult this is, Ms. O'Ryan—"

"Do you?" She rounded on him with surprising anger. "Do you really?"

"Yes." His eyes and voice remained kind. Understanding. "I lost my house in the San Diego fires. And everything in it, including my two dogs."

She stared at him, then closed her eyes and turned away. "I'm sorry." She brought her hands up to her temples. "God, I'm so sorry. I hate this."

She heard footsteps on the gravel and opened her eyes in time see Jack loping toward her. "Sam." He had a frantic look to him as he took her arms in his hands. "I thought you were going to try to go in—"

"I can't. It's not safe." Dully, she introduced the two men, then tuned out their low conversation while she stared at the mess.

There was insurance, she told herself. There was nothing in there she couldn't replace.

Except memories.

"Jesus. Jesus H. Christ." Red showed up in the parking lot, looking shell-shocked. He hadn't tied back his long hair or buttoned his shirt over his long surfer shorts, and, as usual, he wore no shoes. But seeing him standing there was the closest thing to seeing her own parent, and Sam nearly lost it.

"It was the brownies," she whispered, and Red hauled in for a tight hug that blew the air right out of her. That worked for her; she didn't want to breathe, anyway. She fisted her hands in his unbuttoned plaid shirt and held on. "Oh, Red. It's all my fault—"

"Shh." He stroked her hair and she breathed in the scent of the sea, his funky homemade cigarettes and the coconut wax he used on his surfboards. "Thank God you're okay."

Pulling back, she averted her eyes from the ruins. "What about the café?"

"No doubt there's a shitload of work ahead to clean up and rebuild."

"Rebuild." With a little laugh, she shook her head. "I can't do that."

"Why not?"

"Because that takes money."

"Insurance will kick in."

"It'll never kick in enough. I was cheap with the coverage, the cost of replacing everything will kill me—"

"Damn it, I knew you'd be full of excuses." Red dug into the pocket of his surfer shorts and came up with a rolled up piece of paper that he thrust at her.

Sam opened it up and stared at a check drawn from his personal account for a staggering sum of money. "What's this?"

"Every penny of what you've given me over the past five years."

"What? Are you crazy?" She tried to push it back into his hands. "I can't take this."

"Look, get yourself back on your feet. Then you'll start paying me again, and don't think I won't be adding on interest."

She stared at him, not trusting her voice, and he touched her once lightly on the nose, then walked away.

The check in her hand ruffled lightly in the breeze, and she looked down at it, feeling dizzy with gratitude, grief and love.

She wasn't alone. Her gaze lit on Jack, standing there looking right back at her.

She'd never been alone.

That thought was so staggering, she excused herself from everyone including Lorissa, who'd made her way into the blocked-off parking lot and wanted to hug the life right out of her. "I need a minute," she said.

She moved down the stairs to the beach. This strip of sand and rock and bluffs had been a part of her life long before Wild Cherries had been, and it was still there.

Lorissa was still here, up on the dunes.

Red was still there, never judging, never asking anything of her other than to work hard and keep her nose clean.

And then there was Jack.

It was a moment before she realized he was there, too. Not just in spirit, but actually right behind her, respecting her need for privacy but silently offering his strength and hope.

"Sam..."

The torment in his voice had her closing her eyes. "I'm okay. I'm poor and homeless, and feeling a little pathetic, but I'm okay."

"I'd give anything to be able to fix this for you."

Turning her head, she smiled at him through her tears. "I know."

He took one look at her wet eyes and came close, pulling her in for the hug that she desperately needed. "It's really all gone," she whispered, and promising herself it would only be for a moment, clung to him. "Recipes, my mother's china, my favorite bathing suit. They don't even make that kind anymore." A sob escaped her and she didn't try to fight it. There was no need with Jack holding her in a way that told her he'd never let go, not until she wanted him to, which worked for her.

"God, Sam, I'm so sorry—"

"No." She sniffed. "Don't be." She gripped him, buried her face in his neck and inhaled deeply. "It's going to be okay. I'm going to be okay."

Pulling back, he studied her for a long moment before a smile touched his lips. "Yeah. You are."

"It's going to be complicated… Expensive."

"I have way too much money," he said. "Take mine."

That made her laugh through her tears. "No."

"I mean it, I—"

"Jack. That wasn't what I meant by complicated." She'd loved sleeping with him last night. And the way he always looked at her had a way of making breathing difficult. She could tell he was no longer thinking casual, and suddenly she could face that, even if it was more terrifying than losing the café.

"You're not alone, Sam. I want you to know that."

"Yeah. I know."

"I mean it. You have Lorissa and Red. They love you. They'd do anything for you. And you have me. I know you think I'm just your sex slave."

She laughed, as he'd meant her to. But then his smile faded. "I want to be more than your one-night thing, Sam."

Again, she fought for air. "I don't think I've ever met anyone like you."

"Because I tell you like it is?"

"No, Red does that. Lorissa does that. But you…you do something they don't."

"What's that?"

Unable to put it into words, she moved closer to the water. Let her toes dig into the wet sand.

He did the same, and stood next to her, reaching for her hand so that they were connected, but not speaking.

"That's a part of it right there," she said after a moment, her fingers tightening on his. "You don't feel the need to fill up the silence. You can just let me be, you can just let me think."

He looked over at her. "Is there anything else you like about me?"

"Well, there's your body," she said, and laughed when he shifted uncomfortably. "I can't help it. You're a hottie, Jack Knight."

"Yeah, well, same goes. But I was kind of hoping for something more than just…the physical."

She stared at him for a long moment, then turning to face him, took his other hand lightly in her bandaged one, her heart melting when he brought it up to his mouth and gently kissed it. "It's a lot more than physical," she admitted softly, the wind ruffling her hair from her face. "I've never met anyone who's wanted me so much. And I don't mean just sexually. I feel like you really just…want me. *Me*."

"I do," he said. "Very much."

"You never really said, you didn't push—"

Jack shook his head, not sure how to make her understand. "Push? Hell, I could hardly understand the emotions I felt when it came to you. Until last night." He drew in a ragged breath that didn't ease the tightness in his chest. "Last night, I drove up here and had a really bad moment when I saw the flames and not you. Last night, I knew. You're it for me, Sam."

She bent and picked up a rock, tossing it into the ocean. Then searched for another one. Because he could see she was thinking, trying to put things together, he just watched. Waited.

"No one's ever made me think of my future in terms of me and someone," she said after a moment, and turned to eye him as if wanting to see his reaction to that. "Not until you."

He felt the slow smile split his face. "That probably shouldn't make me feel like I just shot the winning point."

Her eyes filled again and his heart cracked. "Oh, Sam…"

"I thought I was so tough, so independent. I thought I had all I needed." She met his gaze, hers shimmering brilliantly. "I was wrong. My life… it was in a rut. Same old comfortable routine, friends, work, everything. Then I met you and things changed. I changed. Suddenly, I wanted more for myself. I *wanted* to think of the future and see myself opening up. Sharing it with someone." She drew a deep breath and looked more nervous than she had last night with fire raining down around her. "I've never wanted forever with someone, Jack, until I met you."

His heart, torn only a moment before, swelled and filled. "Forever?"

"I have no idea what I've gotten myself into, falling like I have for you. I didn't think I was capable of love like this, but that's what it is. I knew it when you burst through the door to save me last night. I knew it when you carried me to your bed with such love in your eyes. I knew it when I woke up this morning wrapped around you." She blew out another big breath. "So." She smiled nervously and stepped back, hugging herself. "Be kind," she whispered.

"You think I'm going to hurt you?" he asked in disbelief.

"You could."

Shaking his head, he sank his fingers into her hair, cradling her head. "Sam, the only intention I have is to love you back." When she only stared at him, he gave a wry grin. "You love me, right?"

"Yes," she whispered. "Yes, I do."

"Good." He lowered his mouth to hers. "My life was in a rut before you, too. I was just existing, maybe even missing basketball more than I admitted to anyone, including myself. But I don't miss anything when I'm with you, Sam. I just feel alive, so alive."

"So…" She smiled tremulously. "What does this mean?"

"Let me put it this way. I want to wake up at the crack of dawn and freeze my ass off in the ocean watching you surf. I want to have you running down my basketball court looking like the sexiest thing I've ever seen, making it so I can't beat you—"

"Are you suggesting you lost because I distracted you?"

"You know damn well that's why I lost, but you're changing the subject. Say yes, Sam."

Her gaze searched his. "To what?"

"To me, to this thing we've got going, to everything."

She laughed a little, looking scared and bewildered and so hopeful he nearly gobbled her up whole.

"Just give you a blind yes?" she asked shakily.

"Uh-huh." His fingers caressed her face. "And we'll fill in all the blanks as they come up."

"You want to wing something this important?" She laughed, then threw herself at him. "Oh my God, that's right up my alley. It's perfect."

"Yeah." He framed her face with his hands. "It is. And so are you."

Epilogue

Eight months later

THE DAY HAD BEEN a good one. Sam had surfed all morning with Lorissa, she'd opened up Wild Cherries Café II in time for a good-sized lunch crowd and now, as the sun set, a pair of headlights came over the bluff. Pulled into her parking lot.

She stood in the café kitchen, her heart starting to pound. Scrunching up her face, she hoped with all her might. Then, and only then, did she slowly open the oven and peek.

"Omigod." Holding her breath, she used her oven mitt to pull out…what looked like a beautifully perfect pan of brownies.

She set the hot pan on the counter and stared at them.

Behind her, Jack came in. "Smells delicious."

"I think I did it," she whispered, her gaze still locked on the brownies. "Come taste, I'm too nervous."

"That's funny." He came up behind her. "Because I'm nervous, too."

Whipping around, she looked at him, concern filling her. They'd been inseparable for eight months. After a few months staying with Lorissa, she'd gotten her own apartment.

She'd spent one night in it.

Then Jack had asked her to move in with him, reminding her she'd given him that blind yes. Since she hadn't needed convincing, she'd gone for it. And while she'd never imagined herself happy in a house she could get lost in, she'd fallen in love with Jack's place the way she had with the man.

He'd been with her every step of the way in the rebuilding of Wild Cherries. She'd been with him when he'd started a new phase in his career…running basketball clinics in the local schools, teaching kids the joy of the game. "What is it?" she asked, stuffing a bite of brownie into his mouth. "Did you get that grant to—"

He chewed. "I got the grant for the district. The kids will have their new courts." He paused, looking startled. *"Yum."*

She had to laugh at his surprise, but then again, she'd been making him taste her brownies for months now, and there'd been some doozies. "You sure they're good? You're not just saying that so you can get lucky?"

"I'm hoping to get lucky with something else entirely." He reached for another bite. "And seriously, these are good. Write down the recipe for this batch." He pulled a small box out of his pocket. "Remember now, you already said yes."

Her heart skipped a beat. "To what?"

"To marrying me." He drew in a deep breath and looked her in the eyes as he opened the box. She caught the flash of light from the beautiful solitaire diamond.

"Be kind," he whispered, echoing the words she'd said to him all those months ago.

She stared down at the incredible ring and felt her throat tighten. "Jack?"

"Yeah?"

"This is better than the brownies."

"Am I getting lucky, Sam?"

"Oh, yeah."

"I don't mean in bed."

"Well, I do. But also right here."

"You're killing me. Tell me quick. Is that a yes, you'll—"

"Yes. Yes, yes, yes…" She threw herself against him, laughing and crying. "Yes to being in love with you, yes to being your wife. Yes, to it all, Jack. *Forever.*"

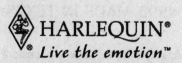